Death Mountain

After the brutal murder of their friend and employer, Matt Stone and Spider McCaw are determined to locate the culprits. Their search leads them to an outlaw hideout, high in the mountains.

The area is called Death Mountain by locals, because no one attempting to pass has ever come back. However, after a running gun battle with the gang, Matt and Spider believe they have located the specific spot of the hideout.

The two friends have to contend not only with the perilous mountain heights, but also with a terrifying menace in a narrow canyon, which is capable of stopping anyone who dares to enter. Can they survive the treacherous journey and bring the killers to justice?

Death Mountain

Dale Brandon

A Black Horse Western

ROBERT HALE · LONDON

© Dale Brandon 2015
First published in Great Britain 2015

ISBN 978-0-7198-1700-7

Robert Hale Limited
Clerkenwell House
Clerkenwell Green
London EC1R 0HT

www.halebooks.com

Typeset by
Derek Doyle & Associates, Shaw Heath
Printed and bound in Great Britain by
CPI Antony Rowe, Chippenham and Eastbourne

CHAPTER 1

A wave of unease swept over Matt Stone when he saw the distant spiral of smoke. Trees blocked most of his view of the valley, but he knew the smoke could only come from the Kern Ranch. Alarmed, he spurred his horse and yelled at his companions. 'Let's ride.'

They followed the trail out of the hills and Matt soon had a full view of the valley. He looked across the flat plain and saw turbulent waves of black smoke rising from the centre of the fire, propelling the dark cloud skyward. After rising several hundred feet, an upper level breeze caught the smoke and spread a thinning layer to the east.

The three riders raced across the valley floor toward the ranch. After several hundred yards, Matt's stronger horse gradually pulled away. He knew from the colour of the smoke that a building was on fire, but it was not until he topped a rise in the trail that he saw it was the ranch house itself. The fire had consumed most of the structure and was beginning to die down for lack of fuel.

Jarrod Kern had built the house the year he moved to Antelope Valley. After struggling those first few years, Kern nearly gave up cattle ranching. Eventually, his ranch became successful and he gradually expanded his operation. In 1874, Kern had hired a pair of rugged, but honest, young cowboys who seemed inseparable. He only needed one new hand at the time, but the pair declined his offer unless both were hired. Kern had taken an instant liking to the two men and hired them on the spot. The new hands were Matt Stone and Spider McCaw. Over the years the three men became close friends. Friendships born out of honesty, loyalty, and trust are indestructible. Such was their relationship.

Concern for Jarrod now occupied Matt's thoughts as he raced down the last incline toward the ranch yard. He drew closer and saw several people standing a safe distance from the fire, but he was still too far away to recognize anyone. Matt wondered how the fire had started. It could have been accidental, but reports of recent outlaw activity in the mountains to the west gave him concern. He had heard of a few isolated incidents in Antelope Valley in recent months, but there had been no such events around the Kern ranch.

He glanced over his shoulder. Spider McCaw and Boyd Cooper were only a hundred yards behind and would provide cover if needed. Matt's horse was drawing heavily and beginning to falter when he reached the yard. The first man he recognized was Sheriff Grimsby; then he saw Nora Higgins, the ranch cook, who had worked for Jarrod for over five years. Cliff Conner, a ranch hand, stood next to Nora. But Matt did not see Jarrod Kern.

When Matt neared the group he saw a tattered blanket covering a body. The smell of burning wood swept through Matt's nostrils as he pulled to a stop and dismounted from his lathered horse. He looked at the solemn group before him and knew he did not have to ask the dead man's identity – the answer was written across each face. It was Jarrod Kern. Matt removed his hat and walked toward the lifeless figure. Agony swept over him. He had lost friends before, but it was always hardest when it came suddenly, without warning. The only things not covered by the blanket were the dead man's boots, the heels blackened with soot.

Sheriff Grimsby broke the uneasy silence. 'It's Jarrod. I'm real sorry.'

Matt paused a moment, then he slowly lifted the top of the blanket. He had assumed his friend had died in the blaze, but there were no burns on the upper body. Puzzled, he turned to Grimsby. 'How'd it happen?'

'I've only been here a few minutes myself. I was on the north road and saw the smoke so I came right over. Nora saw the whole thing and was just starting to tell me what happened.'

Matt turned to the distraught woman. 'Go ahead, Nora.'

The woman lifted her head. 'I heard a commotion and looked out from the barn in time to see riders coming in from two sides. There were eight of them and they had their guns out so I hid.' She hesitated and then continued in a wavering voice. 'Jarrod came out on the porch and they started yelling back and forth.' Nora paused as tears streamed down her face.

Cliff Conner put his arm around her and spoke softly. 'It's OK, Nora. Take your time.'

After gathering herself, she continued. 'I couldn't hear everything but they mentioned Jarrod's safe. They tried to get him to open it for several minutes but he wouldn't go in the house. Then the big man just shot him. He . . . he just kept shooting him until his gun was empty.' Nora stopped to wipe tears from her face. 'They dragged him into the house and set it on fire. Cliff showed up just after they left and barely got Jarrod out.'

'Did you know any of them?' Matt asked.

'I can't see good in the distance, and I was afraid to look out after they shot him. But the big man's voice sounded familiar. He sounded like that man Jarrod ran off for stealing about two years ago.'

Matt's expression changed instantly. 'Caldwell. Jace Caldwell. Is that who you meant?'

Nora thought for a moment. 'I think so, but I can't be positive.'

Sheriff Grimsby stepped closer. 'Nora, could you swear it was him in court?'

She took only a few seconds to answer. 'No, Sheriff, I couldn't do that. I just can't be sure.'

Spider McCaw had been silent, but on hearing Caldwell's name his temper surfaced. 'We should have killed him when you ran him off the ranch, Matt. Now look what he's done.'

'You can't prove it was him,' the sheriff said. He turned to Matt. 'What's all this about Caldwell?'

'He worked here for a short time. Jarrod found out he was stealing cattle so he told him to clear out. I was in the bunkhouse when it happened and I came out just in time to see Caldwell slamming Jarrod against the wall of the house. I jumped in and me and Caldwell were going at it when Jarrod fired a rifle and stopped the fight. Jarrod sent him packing, but Caldwell said he'd be back to settle things. That's the last time I saw him.'

Sheriff Grimsby rubbed his chin. 'We still don't know if it was him.'

'One thing we do know,' Matt replied. 'They're killers and we're going after them.'

Grimsby raised both hands. 'Easy, Matt! We've got to form a posse and do this right.'

'We don't have time, Sheriff. You know they'll head straight for the mountains. If they get up there you'll never find them.' Matt turned away from the group. 'Spider, get some fresh horses. We're leaving right away. Boyd, I want you to ride over to Dickson's place and tell him what happened. Tell him you need food and ammunition. He'll give you anything you need. Get the supplies and head for Eagle Peak. If we can't catch up with them today, we'll meet you at the spring where Clear Creek starts. You know it?'

'Yeah, I know it. I'll leave as soon as I get a fresh horse.'

Sheriff Grimsby was visibly angered. 'You don't have enough men to do this job. Besides, you've got no right to do this on your own.'

Matt looked down at the covered body of Jarrod Kern. 'That's all the right I need, Sheriff. I'm wasting time standing here.' Matt started toward the corral but stopped after a few yards and yelled back at Conner. 'You're in charge. Get word to the boys on the roundup. Call them all in.' While Matt walked toward the corral, a feeling of guilt took hold of him. He had intended to return to the ranch a day earlier but had changed his mind at the last minute. If he had come back yesterday, Jarrod would probably be alive. Matt felt that if he had been here he could have made a difference. When he reached the corral, Spider had finished saddling one horse and was starting on the second. He turned to Matt with anger-filled eyes. 'I'm going to kill that damn Caldwell.'

'I want whoever did it just as bad as you, but we can't prove it was Caldwell.'

'Hell, Matt, you know as well as I do he said he'd get even. Nora thinks it was him. That's good enough for me.'

'Nora isn't sure.'

Matt checked his weapons and mounted. 'They've got a good jump on us so we're going to push hard. Let's go.'

Sheriff Grimsby was still protesting as they rode across the ranch yard. Matt ignored him and struck out across the flats.

The tracks headed straight toward the mountains. Matt kept his eyes on the trail but his mind returned to the image of the tattered blanket covering Jarrod's body. He turned and looked at the remains of the house. The fire had burned out and only a small spiral of smoke rose from the ashes. He again wondered what would have happened if he had come back one day sooner. He turned toward the mountains and did not look back. A rage began to build inside as he rode. He silently vowed to catch the killers and avenge the brutal murder of his friend.

CHAPTER 2

It was late spring in Antelope Valley. There had been few storms in recent months, and the entire region, including the mountain ranges, was in the second year of an increasingly troublesome drought. The higher elevations had obtained some relief, but most of the area remained parched. Matt would have normally paid attention to local range conditions but not today. His thoughts were consumed by his pursuit of the killers. After leaving the ranch, Matt and Spider set an even pace toward the west. The escaping gunmen had made no evident attempts at deception. Their trail led straight across the flats toward the Blue Mountain Range.

They talked little during the first hour, concentrating instead on closing the gap between themselves and the killers. After another half hour, the trail continued in a nearly straight line. Several dust funnels could be seen in the distance, but they saw no other movement. Spider manoeuvred his horse closer to Matt. 'They don't seem to be worried much. They must think they're a mighty tough bunch.'

'They probably figured it would take several hours to form a posse.' Matt paused as he mentally put himself in the position of the gunmen. 'Besides,' he added, 'you can see a long way across this valley. They'll know if anyone is on their trail.'

'I was just thinking,' Spider said. 'There are eight of them and two of us. How are we going to handle this?'

Matt tugged on his hat. 'It wouldn't be wise to take them on in the open, but I'd like to get fairly close before they enter the mountains.'

'Maybe we could get above them and use our rifles?'

'We'll try, but we may just track them. What I really want to know is who they are and where they're from.' Matt paused. 'Then we can settle things.' He gazed across the flats – searching for the gunmen. Five minutes later Matt yelled to Spider. 'Dust – off to the right. You see it?'

'No.'

'A little more to the right. They veered off toward Eagle Peak.'

Spider squinted and looked toward the vast mountain range. 'Yeah, I see it.'

Matt yelled back, 'They're going to spot us any minute. They'll just see the dust at first so they won't know how many are after them for a while. But when they do we've got to be careful.' They had purposely maintained a pace the horses could handle. Matt increased their speed slightly, but not enough to unduly stress the animals. The dust thrown up by the gunmen's horses grew larger, but Matt still could not see the horses or their riders. He was pondering how the outlaws might react once they reached the foothills when he saw the trail of dust separate into two parts.

'Spider, they're splitting up. They probably saw our dust and think there's a bunch of us.'

'Which one do we follow?'

Matt considered their position. 'That group on the right is headed toward Eagle Peak. We've got to meet Cooper at Clear Creek tonight so they'll put us closer to him.' When the outlaws began climbing the hills, Matt saw them for the first time. 'Looks like they split into fours. When we get into those foothills we've got to keep alert for the others in case they figure to double back and put us in a pinch.'

The horses were beginning to labour and needed rest. Matt knew it was unwise to go too much farther without giving them a breather. With the gunmen now out of sight, it was also time for caution. He motioned to Spider and then turned his horse slightly to the north. They veered away from the tracks and entered the foothills several hundred yards north of where they had last seen the outlaws. Matt slowed his horse and turned to Spider. 'I think there's still a trickle of water in Box Creek. We'll rest the horses there, then head south and cut their trail.'

Both men paid close attention to their surroundings as they rode toward the small creek. A few minutes later they reached their destination. They checked the area before dismounting, but found no sign of anyone having been in the vicinity. Neither spoke as the horses drank from the nearly dry creek.

Spider finally broke the silence. 'It's a sad thing. You leave a good man full of life four days ago and the next time you see him he's covered by a blanket. It ain't right.'

Matt was slow to answer. 'I know. The good man is gone but the killer is still alive.' He bent down and picked up a handful of pebbles, then tipped his hat back and slowly tossed the small rocks into the narrow trickle of water. Though he tried, Matt could not get the image of Jarrod's body out of his mind.

Spider shoved himself away from the rock he was leaning on and walked toward his horse. 'Let's get at it.'

Matt threw the last pebble into the creek. 'Spider, they're going to have to rest their horses too, and this creek has the only water for some distance.'

13

'I was just thinking the same thing,' Spider replied. 'But where?'

Matt mounted. 'If they keep going in the same direction they'll hit the water about two miles up. Let's take a chance and follow the ridge above the creek. It'll save time and we might get lucky and get ahead of them. If not, we can always come back and pick up their trail.'

Spider immediately rode across the creek and began to climb the ridge.

Matt shook his head at how impulsive Spider could be. 'You make the quickest damn decisions of any man alive.'

Spider gave a knowing shrug.

The two men used every precaution as they made their way up the ridge. They found good cover among the increasing amounts of brush and large rocks. Trees became more prevalent as they went higher and they soon entered a large stand of pine. When they came within a mile of where they hoped to intersect the outlaws, Matt motioned for Spider to keep on the back side of the ridge.

A quarter mile from their objective they stopped and dismounted. They secured their horses behind a large rock formation and then checked their weapons. They both carried Colt .45 revolvers, but their choice of rifles differed. McCaw used the standard .44–40 twenty inch Winchester Carbine. Matt wanted more range, and had recently purchased a new model Winchester that offered a .45–75 rifle with a twenty-six inch barrel. This rifle was more cumbersome in the saddle, but Matt wanted the power provided by the new model. They retrieved ammunition from their saddlebags and then moved along the ridge on foot. At a predetermined point they stopped and made a final check of the area.

Matt spoke in a low voice. 'If they didn't cut back toward the south they should be along here somewhere. If they are, let's try to get them in a crossfire. But remember:

stay above them and don't forget about the other four. They might show up any time.'

'What if we get separated?'

'If you get in trouble, go higher. Then try to get to Clear Creek. Cooper should be there tonight.' Matt reached into his pocket and pulled out a short length of rawhide, which he inserted into his mouth and slowly began to chew. Matt indulged in the peculiar habit whenever danger was at hand. 'OK, Spider, let's go thin 'em out.' Matt and Spider climbed to the top of the ridge and inspected the ravine below. They could see the narrow creek through the trees, but there was no sign of the gunmen.

'They could have already gone by,' Matt said. 'Let's work our way down and see if their trail went through here.' The two men cautiously manoeuvred down the slope. Halfway down they were able to look through the trees and see the lower section of the creek. Matt suddenly crouched behind a rock and pointed through the trees toward several horses standing near the creek. He watched as four men swung into their saddles and began to move up the ravine.

'We don't have time to set up a crossfire,' Matt said, 'but we'd better spread out some. Work your way up about thirty yards. When the last man goes by me, I'll call 'em out.' Matt searched nearby and found several rock out-croppings along the ridge that offered concealment. He found one to his liking a few yards below. He moved into position and saw Spider go behind large rocks farther up the ridge. He chewed on the rawhide and waited. A picture of the burning ranch house flashed through his mind, and anger grew within him.

The gunmen drew closer.

A point rider was about twenty yards in front of the other three. Matt was motionless as the man rode just below his position. The point glanced up the ridge and then back along the creek. Matt caught a glimpse of the man's face, but he did not recognize him. After the point went by, Matt squinted at the other riders. He was looking for Jace Caldwell, but when the three men came out of the trees he knew the gunman was not in the group. Caldwell was a huge, powerfully built man, but these riders were of average size. Matt began to wonder if Caldwell had actually been with the killers who had raided the Kern ranch.

When the three gunmen were nearly below him, he spit out the rawhide and cocked his rifle. The first and second riders went by, but Matt waited. Finally, when the last man came even with him he yelled out. 'Hands on your hats! Don't try anything!'

The startled men immediately went into action. The first rider spurred his horse and raced up the ravine. The other two drew their guns and fired toward Matt.

Several bullets bit into rocks next to him.

Matt's first shot struck one of the riders on his right side. The man collapsed, but did not fall to the ground. His foot caught in the stirrup and the bolting horse dragged him up the ravine, his head crashing into rocks and stumps as the frightened horse raced ahead. The other man dived behind a group of rocks just as Matt's second shot cut through the air where the man had stood an instant before. Matt fired several rounds into the rocks to keep the man pinned down. One of the bullets might ricochet among the rocks and find its mark.

The heavy boom of rifle and revolver shots sounded from up the ravine. Matt worried that Spider's position was not as good as his own. The two gunmen in the ravine were spread apart and none was directly below Spider when the shooting began. Matt knew he had to dispense with the hidden gunman and then help Spider. He continued to fire into the rocks while moving down the slope.

16

Gunshots reverberated up and down the canyon as he charged forward. After firing the last round from his rifle, he dropped the weapon and reached for his revolver.

The pause caused the outlaw to jump up with fire spewing from his gun. The first bullet flew by Matt's head. Another cut through his shirt, grazing his arm.

Matt's gun erupted. Once, twice – the second shot found the man's forehead. Matt retrieved his rifle and ran up the ravine, but the shooting from above suddenly stopped. The heavy gunfire had caused layers of dense smoke to permeate the ravine. Unable to see anyone, Matt yelled out, 'Spider!' No answer.

He stayed behind cover and squinted in an effort to see, but he saw nothing. After a moment, he repeated the call, 'Spider – you all right?'

A shout came from above. 'I'm OK. The point is still loose but I think he hightailed it out of here.'

'Stay put,' Matt yelled. 'I'll be right up.' He reloaded his weapons and got up. When he started to climb the slope he saw one of the outlaws sprawled on the ground. Matt walked over cautiously, but Spider's shot had been true. The gunman was dead. He checked to see if knew the man but he did not recognize him.

When Matt was halfway up the slope, Spider called to him. 'Was Jace with them?'

'No. Didn't know any of them.'

'He's in that other pack. I know it was him.' Spider seemed intent on placing Caldwell among the killers whether or not he had proof.

Matt's breath came quickly when he reached his friend's position. He paused to catch his breath, then said, 'We've got to find the other four, then we'll know for sure.' He glanced at the sun and calculated their situation. 'We've only got three hours of light. By the time we find their trail and start after them it'll be dark. I think we'd

17

better go on to Clear Creek and meet Cooper. We can stock up on food and ammunition and get some sleep. We'll get an early start tomorrow and stay at it all day.'

Spider wanted to start on the trail right away, but after discussing the options he relented. 'OK, but I want to get up awful early. By the way, how do we handle that mess down there?'

'Grimsby's posse will be along in a few hours. He'll take care of things.'

Aware that the shots may have alerted the other four gunmen, they cautiously made their way back to their horses. They mounted and continued up the ridge. After a steep climb, they struck out across rugged terrain in the direction of Eagle Peak. They were among pine trees now and remained cautious. Matt felt uneasy because the opportunities for ambush were considerable. They crossed two narrow trails but found no sign of fresh tracks.

Night fell quickly in the mountains and temperatures dropped just as suddenly. Darkness made progress difficult but their destination was not far. They saw a few deer as they worked their way through the forest, but no riders. It was after ten o'clock when they approached the spring that gave birth to Clear Creek. They had nearly reached their destination when Matt saw a faint glow. He expected the camp was Cooper's but he had learned long ago to never assume anything. 'Spider, let's go in on foot. You take the left side.' They dismounted and walked toward the glow.

They had nearly reached the rocks when they heard a command off to his right. 'Who's there?' It was Cooper's voice.

'It's Matt. Everything all right?'

'Yeah, come on in.'

Spider turned and headed in the direction they had come from. 'Go ahead, I'll get the horses.'

Matt walked toward the man and extended his hand.

After shaking hands, Cooper said, 'Coffee's hot, supper's ready. I figured you boys would be dragging when you got here.'

'That's a fact, Coop. Thanks.' They walked between the large rocks and stopped next to the fire.

Cooper poured Matt a cup of coffee. 'I went over to Dickson's place like you told me. He was damn sure upset when he heard about Jarrod. He said he'd been expecting some kind of trouble in the valley but nothing like this.'

'He was expecting trouble?'

'Yeah, he said he went over to Benbow about a month ago, and the sheriff told him they were having a helluva problem with a big outlaw gang operating out of the mountains. I guess they've been getting bolder and ranging farther out all the time.'

The new information piqued Matt's curiosity. 'I've passed through Benbow a few times,' he said, 'but I never spent any time there. Who's the sheriff?'

'Potter, Jason Potter. I hear he's a decent sort but it sounds like he's in over his head.'

'Don't know him,' Matt replied.

Spider finished caring for the horses and joined the other two by the fire. 'Howdy, Coop.'

'Hello, Spider. I've got coffee.'

'Thanks. You see anything since you've been here?'

'No, it's been quiet. There are a few tracks around but they're three or four days old.'

Matt considered the new information about the outlaws, then sat his cup down and looked at Cooper. 'What else did Dickson say about this gang?'

'Not much, except they're a clever bunch. They're ruthless, too. They've killed a lot of innocent folks.'

'Yeah,' Matt said, staring into the dark. 'They killed another one today.'

The three men talked for nearly an hour and agreed on a plan for the next few days. Cooper volunteered to stand watch throughout the night so Matt and Spider could rest for the coming ordeal. Cooper would then go back to the ranch and send word to Jarrod's brother, who had a small interest in the ranch. Fortified by the supply of food and ammunition, Matt and Spider would begin an earnest search for the killers the following morning.

CHAPTER 3

They left camp well before dawn. Matt had given considerable thought to the route the killers might take, and concluded there were two likely trails they would take if their destination was the Blue Mountains. Matt intended to intersect the trails at a substantially higher elevation than where they had last seen the second group of gunmen. If they failed to cut the trail, he knew they could backtrack to the same location and start over.

They spent the morning crossing a series of rugged spurs until they came to scattered pines. When they came out of the trees on the edge of a small meadow, Matt slid his rifle from the boot and signalled to Spider. 'The first trail is on the other side of this meadow. We'll stay just inside the trees and work our way over.' After a careful approach, they searched the trail but found no sign of fresh tracks. Matt guided his horse back into the trees and continued south.

Travel became slow and tedious. They crossed several deep ravines that required them to dismount in order to climb up the other side. They had to backtrack on one ridge and go lower in search of a suitable location to cross. At the end of the difficult climb they rested the horses and drank water. Sweating heavily, they sat in silence. Matt's body rested but his mind did not. The anger within continued to grow. After twenty minutes they resumed their search. An hour later, they neared the second trail, which ran nearly parallel to the first. This path was rougher and not often used. They entered a thick growth of mature pine trees and became more cautious. The canopy shielded the afternoon sun, allowing only occasional shafts of hazy light to reach the ground. A breeze from the west caused the pines to make their familiar brushing noise.

There were no other sounds as the two riders approached the trail. They reached a point just above their objective and Matt stopped to listen. If the gunmen did use this trail they would probably have passed by earlier in the day, but Matt was not willing to assume anything. It was his manner to approach every situation expecting trouble. Insight and experience had taught him to always be prepared for anything at any time. Satisfied there was no one in the area, they made their way down to the narrow trail. The pathway was thickly covered with pine needles, and it was difficult to tell if riders had been by recently. Matt dismounted and searched the trail carefully. After a few minutes, he found several markings in the ground where hoofs had kicked up the needles and dug into the earth. The tracks were fresh. Matt swung back into his saddle. 'They've been through here all right.'

'How long?'

'I'd guess they've got about four hours on us. They probably camped down the mountain last night and came through here before noon.'

'I doubt if we can catch them today,' Spider said. 'But we can sure as hell cut the distance.'

Matt took the lead as they rode along the narrow trail. He intended to push as hard as was prudent for the first hour or two and then reduce the pace. As they rode deeper into the mountains they would be entering unfamiliar terrain. Thus, he intended to become more wary with each passing mile. They made good progress the rest of the day. At sunset, he guided his horse off the path and climbed to a large rock formation overlooking the trail. They dismounted, cared for their horses, and set up camp. Although the location of their camp was relatively safe they chose not to build a fire. One mistake could cost them their lives.

The two men alternated watch duty during an uneventful night. They had a cold breakfast and resumed their search an hour before sunrise. At first light, Matt stopped to inspect the trail where it passed over an area of soft dirt. After careful scrutiny, he turned to Spider. 'These weren't made this morning. They probably came through here late last night. If they set up camp they could be real close.' Matt stuck a piece of rawhide in his mouth and pulled his Winchester from the boot. He was deep in thought as he slowly chewed on the strip of hide. 'It's rugged,' he said looking over the terrain. 'I think we'd best move off the trail for a while.'

'Yeah,' Spider replied. 'I've got a feeling they're lazy. If they didn't push it they could be anywhere along here.'

Matt checked both sides of the trail and found the best access on their right. He guided his horse through large pines and climbed halfway up the nearby ridge. When not obscured by trees they could easily see the trail. They rode along the ridge on a course parallel to that of the path below. After less than an hour Matt motioned to Spider, pulled to a stop, and pointed through the trees to a faint thread of smoke. They dismounted and moved to a protected spot that offered a better view. They watched for several minutes, but there was no sign of movement.

Matt spoke in a low voice. 'Looks like they threw dirt on the fire but it didn't go all the way out. I think it's been smouldering for a while.'

'Let's have a look.'

They spread apart and rode slowly down to the small fire. Matt dismounted and inspected the campsite while Spider checked for tracks. After his examination, Matt walked toward the trail.

'Over here,' Spider said. 'It looks like there were about four of 'em.'

'It's them. I'm sure of it.'

'They're not far ahead of us. How do you want to handle it?'

Matt thought a moment. 'This is ambush country sure as hell. We've got to be patient and just keep tracking them.'

Spider followed the trail with his eyes. 'Yeah, there's dozens of places along here where they could jump us. I'd like to get right after them but I know you're right.'

'We'd best go slow through these trees.' Matt followed the trail until the sun was high overhead, then he decided to rest briefly and care for the horses. After twenty minutes, they resumed travel and made their way deeper into the Blue Mountain range. The terrain gradually changed. They left the heavy trees and found a rugged mountain wall on their right. Matt found numerous tracks in each direction. Signs of cattle and horses were everywhere, many of the markings were fresh. The tracks they followed soon disappeared into the middle of a small herd of cattle and it became impossible to determine in what direction the gunmen had fled.

Spider rode about, surveying the ground, cursing in a low tone.

After studying the area, Matt guided his horse next to Spider's. 'It looks like they went straight through the cattle toward the wall. They had to have gone out one end or the other. You swing off to the right and check that way.'

'Too damn many tracks,' Spider muttered as he rode away.

Matt went along the edge of the steep wall. He soon passed the cattle and found himself in an area covered with rock. The large imbedded rocks could easily conceal the passage of riders. He dismounted and searched for markings but was disappointed when he found abrasions all over the rocks. It was obvious many riders had been over the area at various times, but it was impossible to determine if any had been this way today. He mounted and pondered the strange location. It was almost as if the area was deliberately prepared to confuse trackers. He searched a little longer, then rode back toward where he left Spider. He approached the rendezvous point and saw Spider come out of the trees. Matt called out.

'What'd you find?'

'Not a thing,' Spider said. 'There are a few old horse tracks up that way but mostly cattle. There's a narrow canyon that cuts into the mountain but, for some reason, there were no tracks of any kind going into the canyon. All I saw was one helluva big rattlesnake. He spooked my horse good. Biggest damn snake I ever saw.' Spider shook his head. 'I also saw a dead steer, all swollen up. Looked like a rattler got him in the head while he was grazing.'

'This is a strange set-up. I can't figure how those men just disappeared.' Matt looked over the area. 'I found a large section of rock below. That's the only way they could have gone.'

'I've got a funny feeling about this place,' Spider replied.

'Yeah, so do I.'

'They have to leave the rocks somewhere.'

Matt glanced around. 'Let's keep looking.' They scoured the rocks for nearly an hour without finding any sign of fresh tracks. The terrain soon became impassable, forcing them to suspend efforts in that direction. Puzzled, they finally stopped on a high point with a good view of the mountainous terrain. 'What do you think?' Matt asked.

'I don't know. I'm damn sure at a loss.'

'That makes two of us. About the only thing I can figure is that they're headed down the mountain. How far do you think it is to Benbow?'

'Benbow? Less than a day's ride.'

Matt scanned the area. 'Let's sweep through the trees below here. We might get lucky and pick up their trail. If not, we'll go into Benbow and have a look. The sheriff should know a lot more about this bunch than we do.'

Spider shook his dead. 'I still can't figure how we missed 'em.'

The two men did not return to the trail. Instead, they searched through the pines as they gradually made their way down the mountain. They came across numerous markings, but none were the fresh tracks of four riders. In late afternoon, they came to an area where the trees thinned considerably and large rock outcroppings abounded. They found two small mining tunnels, but there was no sign of anyone being there recently. They inspected the second tunnel and then resumed their journey to Benbow. After only a few minutes, Matt spotted a single man. 'Spider, through the trees.'

'I see him.'

The man was seated beside a small campfire. 'It seems odd that a man would ride through this country alone,' Matt said. 'It may be a trap.' They checked the surrounding area but saw nothing. 'Let's move into the trees. We'll watch him a while, then go in slow.'

The man had been seated with his back to the riders, but just as they started toward the trees the man stood up and looked around. When he spotted them, he bolted for his horse. He nearly fell as he ran but he quickly mounted and rode out of sight.

'Seems mighty nervous,' Spider said.

'Let's check the campsite to see if he was alone, then we'll go after him. But keep an eye out. This could still be a set up.' They rode into better cover and spread apart. With rifles ready, they moved toward the campsite. A search of the camp showed the man had not been alone. At least two or three other men had left gear on the ground.

Matt felt uneasy. 'I don't like it. Let's get to a safer spot.' He started toward the trees and called to Spider, 'Keep a little distance between us.'

Spider swung out about fifteen yards and somewhat ahead of Matt. When Matt reached the edge of the campsite he pulled his horse to a sudden stop. He heard something that sounded out of place. He listened but the sound stopped.

'Spider, hold up.' After a moment, he heard a faint cry. Someone was calling for help off to his right. The voice cried out again. The sound of despair from the call was real, someone was in serious trou-ble. Matt rode about thirty yards to his right and stopped next to a vertical mine shaft. He dismounted with his rifle ready and cautiously went to the edge of the pit.

He stared down in disbelief.

CHAPTER 4

A young girl clung to a small ledge in the deep shaft. Her dress was dirty and torn, and Matt thought she could only have been eight or nine years old.

The girl looked up. 'Help me, Mister ... please help me.'

'Don't worry, we'll get you out.' He turned and saw Spider riding toward him.

'What's wrong?'

'You won't believe it. Bring a rope.'

Spider came to the edge of the pit and looked down. 'Is she all right?'

'I think so, but let's get her out of there.' Matt took the rope and put the loop around his body, then he handed the other end to his partner. 'Wrap it around that stump and lower me down, but keep your eyes peeled.' Matt lowered himself about ten feet to the ledge. He turned and reached for the girl, but she seemed unsure. She started to cry. He crouched before her and put his hands on her shoulders. 'Listen to me. We're friends. We're not going to hurt you. Do you understand? We're friends.'

The girl's cries turned to sobs as she looked into his face.

As she stared at him, Matt sensed her terror slowly easing. 'I'm going to put this rope around you and help you up. My partner will lift you the rest of the way out. You'll be OK. I promise.'

With that, the girl suddenly put her arms around Matt and clung to him.

He felt overwhelmed by the girl's sudden show of trust, but as she held on to him he also knew they should leave the area quickly. He looked toward the top of the hole. 'Comin' up.' He lifted the girl and Spider pulled her out of the shaft. After a few seconds, the rope dropped and Matt climbed from the pit. He stepped away from the shaft and spoke to the girl. 'I want you to tell me all about this, but first we've got to get you somewhere safe. Do you understand?'

'Y-yes.'

Matt swung into his saddle, then Spider lifted the girl up behind him. 'Put your arms around me and hold tight. If we get into trouble you're going to have to hang on with all your strength. Don't forget.'

'I won't.'

'What's your name?'

'Katherine, but everyone calls me Katie.'

'All right, Katie. Hold on.'

Spider led the way into the trees. They moved cautiously at first, then picked up the pace and rode for nearly two hours without incident. It was about an hour before sunset when Matt pulled up next to Spider. 'We'd better find a good spot and set up camp.'

Spider nodded and began to search the terrain as they rode on slowly. Twenty minutes later, he swerved to his right and began to climb a small ridge. They stopped at a protected point on the slope among large rocks.

Matt helped Katie down and dismounted. They made the girl comfortable, then Matt sat next to her. 'Katie, I want you to tell us what happened. Go slow and try to remember everything.'

Katie seemed to be collecting her thoughts so she said nothing for a moment. There was a look of sadness on her face as she sat motionless, staring forward. She finally began. 'I go riding a lot with Uncle Blake. We went out the day before yesterday and were stopped by three men. They got into an argument with Uncle Blake and—' Katie began to sob.

Matt put his arm around her and spoke in a soft voice. 'It's all right, Katie. Take your time.'

After a few minutes, she tried again. 'They sh . . . shot Uncle Blake and grabbed my reins.' Katie wiped tears from her eyes as she spoke. 'Then they took me into the mountains and put me in that awful hole.'

'Did any other men come to the camp?'

'No, but I think they were waiting for someone.'

'Did they say his name?'

'No.'

'What else did you hear?'

'I heard them say they were going to get money from my pa.'

Spider bent down in front of the girl. 'Where do you live, Katie?'

'On my daddy's ranch. It's in Pine Valley.'

'What's your last name?' Spider asked.

'Colby.'

Matt recognized the name. 'Major Colby of the Box C?'

'Yes, he's my daddy.'

Matt and Spider exchanged glances. The Box C was a large, well-known ranch. Although neither had met Major Colby, Matt knew the name, as did most ranchers in the region. Colby ran a solid and respected operation. Matt stood and looked down the slope before speaking. 'We've heard of your father, Katie, and we'll see that you get home safely.'

'I believe you, Mister. What's your name?'

'I'm Matt Stone and this is Spider McCaw.'

Katie had a puzzled expression on her face. 'Spider? His name is Spider?'

McCaw stood up and turned over a stone with his boot. 'Well, Katie, my real name is Jack, but everyone calls me Spider whether I like it or not.'

'Mr McCaw, I never heard of anyone named Spider before.'

Matt chuckled. 'I'll bet you're hungry.'

'I'm very hungry, Mr Stone.'

'Well, Katie, we'll rustle up supper; then I want you to get some sleep.'

'You stay with her,' Spider said. 'I'll take care of the grub.'

While Spider began preparations, Matt asked the girl several questions. After a few moments he sensed she wanted to talk about something else. She had obviously been through a difficult experience. When Matt saw Katie glance toward Spider, he said, 'So you think his name is funny, huh?'

'Yes, I do.'

'Would you like to hear how he got that name?'

'Sure.'

Matt shifted to a more comfortable spot. 'Well, it all started when he was a young boy. He lived in an orphanage and had to share a room with a lot of other orphans. He told me he was sleeping in the top bunk when something woke him up. It seems that a poisonous spider had come down from the ceiling on its web and landed in his open mouth. He felt something crawling around on his tongue and tried to spit it out, but the spider bit him.'

Katie grimaced. '*Inside* his mouth?'

'Yes. He was very sick for several days, and his tongue had swollen so large he couldn't eat. He could hardly breathe and nearly died. To this day he'll fight any three men or beasts, but he's scared to death of spiders.'

'Then why does he use *that* name?'

'He didn't want to, but that's the only name the other boys would use. He finally gave up and the name has stuck with him ever since.'

Katie thought for a moment. 'Is that the truth, Mr Stone?'

'It's the honest truth.'

By the time the meal was ready, Katie seemed at ease with her new friends. Matt picked up a plate of food and handed it to Katie, then he moved away and sat with his back against a large rock. Everyone began to eat. After a few minutes, Katie got up and walked over to Matt and then sat next to him. She did not say anything, but she ate the rest of her meal seated very close to him.

After supper, Matt took the first watch as Spider and the girl slept. He gave Katie his bed-roll to protect her from the night air. Later, he would wake Spider and exchange places with him. During his watch, he heard nothing but a few animals. They were up at dawn, and after a small breakfast, they set out for Benbow. Matt decided to stay in the trees for the first two hours. When they were within half a day's ride to town he felt it would be safe to use one of the trails. When they finally cut the trail, he signalled for Spider to pick up the pace. After an hour they came to a large meadow. The pathway cut across the centre, then skirted the northern edge before disappearing in the trees. Halfway across the meadow Matt suddenly stopped. 'Movement in the trees. Let's head for the other side.'

Just as they started across the clearing, several riders appeared on that side. Matt turned and looked back. Five riders came out of the trees from the north side. Three more suddenly appeared on the trail at the end of the meadow. Matt started to turn and make a run in the direction that they had come but realized he could not. If gunfire erupted, the girl would be in serious danger. Both men had already pulled their Winchesters. Matt yelled at Spider. 'You face that bunch on the left. I'll take the one on the right. Keep your rifle on them but hold your fire.'

Katie yelled out. 'It's the sheriff. It's Sheriff Potter.'

Matt was relieved and lowered his rifle as the riders approached. 'Which one is Sheriff Potter?'

'Over there . . . the one in front.'

Katie pointed to the lead rider who was now less than a hundred feet away. Matt had never seen the man before. Sheriff Potter appeared to be in his mid-forties. A large black moustache, speckled with grey, was the predominant feature on his face. As the sheriff drew closer, Matt noticed a stern, no-nonsense look in the man's face.

Matt spoke as the men pulled to a stop. 'Sheriff, I—'

The sheriff interrupted with a loud command. 'Drop your guns. Now!'

They were surrounded. Matt looked around and saw that every rider had a gun levelled on them, and he realized that the posse had found them with the girl and probably took them for kidnappers and killers. He raised his left hand, palm out. 'Hold on, Sheriff. Let me explain.'

Sheriff Potter spoke briskly, 'I'm not telling you again. Drop your guns.'

The click of several hammers being cocked could be heard all around.

Matt glanced at Spider. 'We best do as he says.' They dropped their weapons.

The sheriff pulled his horse closer and called orders to his men, 'Carson, get the Colby girl away from them. Buck, tie their hands.'

Spider broke his silence. 'You're making a mistake, Sheriff.'

'I want you two fellas to shut up. You can do your

talking in town, but for now, you damn sure had better keep quiet.'

One of the riders yelled out. 'Let's string them up right here.'

The sheriff turned a harsh stare toward the man. 'Harley, you know I won't stand for that kind of talk. I'll not hear any more of it.' His eyes scanned the group. 'From anyone.' He then turned to the man who had Katie. 'Carson, take two men and get Katie back to the Major.'

The rider, who had taken Katie a short distance away from the group, spoke up. 'Right away, Sheriff.'

When Katie saw one of the men start to tie Matt's hands she knew something was wrong. 'I've got to talk to the sheriff,' she pleaded.

'Not now, Katie,' the rider said. 'We've got to get you safely away from here.'

Katie looked back from her horse as the three men guarding her struck out for the trail. She pleaded again. 'But, Mister—!'

'Not now, Katie. You can talk to him tomorrow.'

Concern etched across Katie's face as she looked back before disappearing into the trees.

CHAPTER 5

It was mid-afternoon when the posse reached the outskirts of Benbow. During the journey, Matt had made another attempt to speak to the sheriff but his effort had failed. He had been sternly warned that his mouth would be stuffed with a bandana if he did not keep quiet. The narrow road passed a few scattered houses, then gradually widened into a bustling street that ran through the centre of town. Matt noticed the harsh stares of both men and women on the boardwalk. Almost everyone in Benbow had known and liked Blake Colby, and everyone knew the posse had been formed to find Katherine Colby and bring in Blake's killers.

As the riders moved slowly up the main street, excited youngsters ran along the walkway informing the towns-people as they went. An increasing number of citizens came out of shops to observe the procession. Some of the onlookers spoke out harshly; others simply stared at the men. The jail was about a hundred yards away when they approached the Dog Head Saloon. Four riders came around a corner and pulled up in front of the saloon. A large man stepped down from his horse and looked at the approaching posse.

Matt instantly recognized the man. It was Jace Caldwell.

Spider saw the gunman in the same instant and became

enraged. Here was the very man he sought, but he was now unable to do anything. Spider glanced at Matt. 'You see him?'

'Yeah, I see him. You notice there are *four* of them?'

A smile appeared on Caldwell's face when he recognized the two captives. 'Well, look what we've got here. You boys are a long way from home.'

Matt shot a cold look at Caldwell, but said nothing as he was not in a position to back his words – he had more pressing problems.

Caldwell evidently expected more of a reaction. Receiving none, he spoke again in a louder voice. 'You boys get caught stealing horses – or was it for raping young girls?'

Spider's temper exploded. He dug his spurs into his horse and headed straight toward the outspoken gunman. Caldwell was big and powerful but he was not quick. He attempted to step to the side and avoid the horse but he was too late. The animal's chest struck the gunman's side and sent him sprawling. Caldwell was furious. He sent forth a shower of curses as he sprang to his feet and started to draw his pistol.

The thunderous boom of a gunshot echoed through the street. Sheriff Potter rode up to the two men with his revolver drawn, smoke curling out of the barrel. 'That's enough,' he yelled. 'Jace, if you're going into the saloon, then get on with it. I don't want to hear any more from you.'

Caldwell stood for a second, then slowly removed his hand from the gun butt. 'Sheriff,' he yelled. 'When the time comes you're gonna hear plenty from me.' He gave the sheriff an icy stare, then walked into the saloon. The other three gunmen followed close behind.

Even though Spider's hands were tied he had managed to guide his horse into Caldwell. After the incident, two members of the posse rode over and took control of his horse. The sheriff yelled out. 'Get them off the street and put them in jail.' Matt and Spider were hastened to the jail and locked up. There was general commotion and loud voices coming from the sheriff's office for over an hour, but the two men were left alone in their cells.

After the excitement died down the sheriff opened the heavy wooden door separating his office from the cells. He walked over to a barred window at the far end of the room. 'We've got some angry folks out there. They'd like to hang you boys.'

Matt stood and walked to the cell door. 'Sheriff—'

'Hold on, Son,' the sheriff interrupted. 'You've been wanting to tell your side of things and now's your chance, but I can tell when a man's lying so don't make a fool of yourself.'

Matt figured the sheriff was bluffing about his abilities, but it didn't matter. The truth was all he intended to give. When Matt told the sheriff of Jarrod Kern's death the lawman let out an audible groan.

Potter looked at Matt with a painful expression. 'Jarrod and I worked on the same spread together. It must have been twenty years ago.' The sheriff was going back in time. It could be seen in his face. 'I haven't seen much of him in recent years . . . but he was a good friend.'

Matt explained how Caldwell had been run off the Kern ranch and of his vow to get even with Jarrod. He also indicated that a witness thought it might have been Caldwell who shot Jarrod, but he admitted she was not positive.

Potter stated flatly that they offered no proof.

Matt had nearly finished relating the events of the past few days when voices sounded from the office, then someone knocked on the door.

'Sheriff, it's Colby.'

Potter opened the door. 'Howdy, Major. I'm sure glad we got little Katie back safe.'

A man in his late fifties came through the door with his hat in his hand. His head was covered with long, neatly combed, silver hair. A large white moustache accented his pleasant face. He stood straight and had a look of health about him. 'Katie is the reason I'm here,' Colby said. 'She told me the whole story.' He turned toward the cell. 'These men are innocent – they helped her escape. I rushed into town as soon as I found out.'

'You know,' the sheriff said, 'when they told me they worked for Jarrod Kern I began to wonder about them. Jarrod would never have kept outlaws on his payroll.' The sheriff related the news of Kern's death and other events as told by Matt.

'Well, Sheriff,' Colby said. 'Let's not just stand around. Get them out of there.'

After the sheriff opened the cell door, Major Colby extended his hand, a warm smile crossed his face. 'I want to thank you men. I owe you a great deal.' The major turned and walked to the office door. 'You've got a friend out here who wants to see you.'

When Matt walked through the door, Katie rushed across the room with her arms spread apart. Matt bent down to accept the girl's hug. She was a delightful girl who displayed a wonderful innocence. Matt became aware of others in the room and looked over Katie's shoulder toward a young woman. His gaze met hers and held. Matt was stunned by the overall appearance of the woman. He rose and continued to look at her. The woman appeared to be about twenty-two years old. Her sun-washed, blonde hair seemed to catch every ray of light. The hair was swept back from her face and shaped into a roll in the back. But what attracted Matt was an uncommon radiance in her face. Her skin carried a faint golden tone and she exuded a fresh look. Her blue eyes were alive and joyful.

Katie looked toward the woman. 'Mr Stone, this is my sister, Laura.' Katie turned back to the two men. 'Laura, this is Mr Stone and Mr McCaw.' She giggled and pointed at Spider. 'You'll never guess what his first name is.' Katie couldn't wait for her sister to answer. 'It's Spider. Have you ever heard of anyone called Spider?'

'Why, no . . . no, I haven't.'

Spider spoke first. 'Howdy, Miss.'

'Hello, Mr McCaw.'

Matt put his arm around Katie. 'I'm pleased to meet you, Laura. You've got a wonderful little sister here.'

'Yes, I know.' Laura said with her gaze directly on Matt. 'We were terribly afraid we'd lost her. My Dad and I don't know how to thank you.'

'We were happy to have been able to help.'

Major Colby stepped forward. 'We can start by inviting these fine men to supper. It's too late today, but I'll put you up in the hotel tonight and you can come out to the ranch tomorrow afternoon. After the last few days you could probably use a good night's sleep. Tomorrow, we'll have a supper in your honour to celebrate Katie's safe return.' He looked at his daughter and winked. 'It also happens to be her ninth birthday.'

Spider had been watching Matt's reaction to the woman. 'We'll be glad to come by tomorrow, Major,' he said. 'Thanks for the invite.'

Major Colby walked to the door, opened it, and called to someone outside. 'Henry, go over to the hotel and fix these men up with rooms.' Everyone left the sheriff's office in good spirits. After talking for several minutes, the Colbys got into a wagon and bid everyone goodbye.

Spider started across the street, but Matt could not resist looking back at the departing wagon. He turned just in time to see Laura turn and look toward him. Again,

39

their gazes met and held. In that instant, he experienced a sensation unlike any he had ever felt. It was another minute before he realized Spider was in full laughter.

'What's so funny?'

'You are,' Spider answered. 'You should see yourself. You've been lassoed and reeled in and don't even know it.'

To Matt's dismay, Spider burst into laughter again. Matt tried to ignore his friend as they walked across the street, but he could not resist turning to look at the departing wagon once more. When they reached the opposite boardwalk, Spider's temperament changed instantly. Standing outside the Dog Head Saloon was one of the three gunmen who entered town with Jace Caldwell.

'Matt—'

'I see him.'

'I could sure use a whiskey,' Spider said. His gaze remained on the gunman.

Matt looked toward the saloon door. 'Yeah, so could I.'

They walked toward the batwing doors in a confident manner.

The lone gunmen finished a cigarette and flipped it into the street. When Matt reached the doors, the gunman looked up and said, 'I wouldn't go in there if I were you, Mister.'

'You ain't me,' Matt answered as he walked through the doors. Spider followed close behind. Matt entered the large room and looked around. To his right was a long bar where six men stood. Two were quite drunk but they seemed harmless. A black on white sign was centred above the bar. It read:

GUNS MUST BE CHECKED IN ALL SALOONS
BY ORDER OF SHERIFF POTTER.

There were a series of pegs along the back wall. Half of

them were covered by a variety of holsters and weapons. Hog-legs, Peacemakers, Remington Army models. All types of revolvers seemed to be represented along the wall. Matt looked around and noticed that everyone had pegged their weapons. The rule was obviously enforced. Another quick glance located Jace Caldwell and his two companions seated at a table against the left wall. Caldwell acted as though he had not seen them enter the saloon. Matt walked to the rear of the room, unbuckled his holster, and handed it over. Spider followed suit.

As soon as they hung up their guns and moved away, Caldwell turned and looked straight at Matt. His loud, deep voice carried easily across the noisy saloon. 'They already let you boys off for violatin' that little girl?'

The words struck with the force of a thunderbolt. All eyes turned toward Matt as silence spread over the room.

CHAPTER 6

Several tables separated the two men. Matt looked directly at the burly gunman, his voice direct and stern. 'The fact is we saved Katie's life. And I've got another fact for you, Caldwell.'

'Yeah, well, I'm listening,' the gunman answered in a drawn-out, sarcastic tone.

Matt paused a few seconds to insure that his next words would have full impact. He raised his voice. 'It took eight of you *girls* to kill one unarmed man, and we're going to stick around until we prove it.'

He had barely finished when Caldwell stood up and flung a whiskey bottle straight at him. Matt ducked; the bottle sailed over his head and crashed into the wall behind the bar. He rose up in time to see Caldwell coming toward him in a rage. Matt threw a chair aside to meet the oncoming rush. Out of the corner of his eye he saw Spider heading toward the other two gunmen. They were in for a bloody fight.

The glance toward the others was a mistake. Before Matt was able to get fully set, Caldwell's head hit him square in the chest, causing him to stumble backwards and crash against the bar. Caldwell was a tall, powerfully built man, and Matt felt the full extent of his force from the charge. Matt slumped to a sitting position against the bar and was trying to get up when he saw Caldwell's right boot being drawn back for a full kick. Matt rolled to his right just as the man's boot slammed into the wooden frame where his head had rested a split second before. Caldwell cursed and turned to face his prey.

Matt jumped to his feet and swung a vicious right that caught his opponent square on the chin. The big gunman staggered slightly, but showed no other effects from the solid blow. Matt followed with a quick left that landed in the centre of the outlaw's face. A spurt of blood shot from Caldwell's nose, but again, he showed no other effects from the punch. Before Matt could swing again, the big man rushed at him and applied a bear hug. The burly outlaw was obviously best in close quarters. Caldwell applied tremendous pressure to Matt's torso. At the same time the gunman moved his head back, then thrust it forward, slamming his forehead squarely against Matt's head. The blow was sudden and powerful. Caldwell struck again in the same manner. The smashing blows seemed to have no effect on the man delivering them, but they were having a tremendous impact on Matt. The second blow to Matt's head caused a sudden cloud of darkness to streak across his vision. He could see nothing to the side and everything in front of him seemed out of focus. He had to free himself or the powerful man would soon have him down and beat him to death.

Before Caldwell could strike again, Matt angled his right foot to the side and raised his boot as high as he could. He then put his entire effort into slamming his foot straight down. The heel of his boot scraped the edge of Caldwell's shins and plunged down on top of the man's in-step. The strength of the blow forced Caldwell to release his smothering grip. The big man showed his first sign of pain as he grimaced and grabbed his foot. Matt instantly swung a solid right hand uppercut under the chin. Caldwell fell on the edge of a table, then rolled over and landed on the floor.

Matt thought he had delivered the decisive blow, but Caldwell quickly rose to his feet. Matt swung a roundhouse right hand at the man's chin, but knew he had made a mistake a split second after he initiated the blow. The wide, swinging punch would take too long to find its mark. Caldwell threw up his left arm to block the blow. At the same instant, he sent a powerful right straight at Matt's jaw. The impact of the crushing blow could be felt all over the room. The punch was so forceful that Matt's feet were lifted into the air before he landed on his back. Again, a faint black cloud covered his field of vision. Even in his groggy state, Matt knew he could not beat this huge man by trading punches. He raised himself to his elbows and shook his head.

A voice yelled out from somewhere in the room. 'Look out!'

The blackness had faded slightly and he saw Caldwell raising a chair high over his head. Matt rolled to one side just before the chair smashed into the floor. He sprang up and swung a hard left fist into the stomach. Caldwell emitted a sudden loud groan and slumped forward slightly, gasping for air. That's his weak spot, Matt thought. *His gut – pound at his gut.* Matt followed the punch with a solid right to the stomach. Again, the huge man let out an audible groan. Matt side-stepped a weak right hand and threw a succession of hard blows into the same spot. Caldwell was now bent over and gasping for air. Matt put all of his strength into a thunderous right hand uppercut that caught the gunman on the sweet spot under his chin. The big man keeled over backwards and crashed to the floor. This time, he did not move. Matt knew there had been two other gunmen in the saloon and one more at the front entrance. He wondered why the others had not entered the fight as he looked around the room.

Spider had one of the men up against a wall. His fists were a blur. Spider landed punch after punch on his much taller opponent, then he suddenly backed away and watched as the man slid down the wall. The man was unconscious before he hit the floor. Matt watched as Spider turned toward him and nearly tripped over another of the gunmen who he had dispensed with moments before. Matt had seen Spider in action many times, but he was always amazed at the speed, power, and intensity of his friend. Pound for pound, Spider McCaw was the best fighter he had ever seen.

But there were four gunmen. Matt turned toward the front doors prepared for any eventuality. The fourth man was standing just inside the room. Two cowhands stood with him – one on either side. When Matt entered the saloon, the fourth man had been outside with his gun belt still on, but the man's gun was now missing. Matt glanced at the cowboys standing next to the man. He recognized neither man, but he noticed one of them had a revolver stuck under his belt. They had obviously disarmed the fourth man and kept him from interfering in the fight. Matt walked toward the door.

The man on his left put out his hand. 'We're from the Box C,' the man said. 'We heard what you did for Katie and we figured the least we could do was to see that you had a fair scrap. We weren't about to let somebody back-shoot you.'

Matt shook hands with the men. 'Thanks, we appreciate it. I'm Matt Stone and this is Spider McCaw.'

'I'm Fuzzy Thurman,' the man on the left said, 'and this

is Gus Knox. We've worked for the major for over five years now, and we've watched little Katie grow up. She's a fine girl and we'd sure hated to have lost her.'

Spider shook hands and thanked the two men before turning to Matt. 'I think I could use that whiskey now.'

'You boys sort of wrecked this place,' Fuzzy said. 'But if you'll walk down the street with us we'd like to buy you that drink.'

'Much obliged,' Spider answered. 'Matt, I'll get our guns.'

When Spider returned with their gun belts, Thurman emptied the cartridges from the pistol in his belt, and then threw the weapon on the floor. The four men walked down the street to another saloon. Matt took an instant liking to the Box C men as they talked over their whiskey. Thurman was a tall, thin man in his late thirties. He had lost considerable hair and what remained of his brown hair was short and coarse. He had a quick smile and seemed as honest as they come. Knox was more subdued. He was a little taller than Spider, but not as stocky. He chewed tobacco constantly and seemed to watch every passerby closely. He said little, but he seemed a decent sort. Matt thought he was probably a hard-working and loyal hand. During their conversation they learned that the Box C was the largest outfit in the area, and that Major Colby was a consistently fair man who was well respected throughout the region.

After their talk with the Box C hands, Matt and Spider went to the hotel, looking forward to their first good night's sleep in several days. Before going to bed, Matt tended to the injuries he obtained during the fight. He did not look as bad as he expected, except for a welt on his forehead that seemed to grow larger with each passing minute.

The following morning, the two men bathed, ate break-fast, and became acquainted with Benbow. Word about Katie's rescue had spread fast, and they experienced a much different reception from the townspeople than when they had first entered town as prisoners. Many of the citizens went out of their way to apologize for their behaviour of the previous day, and Matt had a good feeling about the people he met. After purchasing a birthday gift for Katie, Matt and Spider set out for the Box C Ranch. It was after four o'clock when they approached the Colby Ranch. They crossed a wooden bridge over a small creek and saw a small figure sitting on top of the gate that opened into the ranch yard. When they got closer, a young girl stood up on one of the wooden rails and began waving at them.

A smile crossed Matt's face. 'It's Katie. Looks like we've got a friend for life.'

'She's a real sweet kid,' Spider offered. He paused, then added with a chuckle. 'She's got an real sweet sister, too.'

Matt started to say something, but he knew it was a hopeless cause. They drew closer to Katie and saw her now familiar curly brown hair and freckled nose. When they reached her they broke into broad smiles. 'Well, hello, Katie,' Matt said. 'You look pretty today.'

Katie smiled and said happily, 'It's my birthday.'

When Matt reached the gate he held his arm out to help her on to his horse. 'Well, we're going to make sure you have a good one.' When they were nearly at the house, Major Colby came through the front door. He flashed a sincere smile and greeted them warmly. Matt thought it would be hard to not like Colby.

'Katie,' the major said, 'why don't you go inside and check on supper. I want to show our guests around.' Colby walked them around the yard and talked about a number of things, but mostly ranching and the drought. He also showed them his prize horses, including a magnificent black stallion he called Mesquite.

After thirty minutes, the supper bell rang and the men made their way toward the house.

Matt had not seen Laura until they entered the main room of the large house. She came through a doorway wearing a white dress with a large yellow ribbon cinched around her waist. Her feminine curves could not go unnoticed. Her hair was down and flowed over her shoulders. Her appearance stunned Matt. She possessed the same bright freshness he had seen before, but the dress and her cascading hair brought out her true beauty. The small group conversed for several minutes before going into the dining room. Matt noticed that Laura was polite, but she did not look at him in the same way she had on the previous day. She seemed to be carefully avoiding direct eye contact. He was confused and began to think that he had read something into the previous meeting that was not really there.

Before they entered the dining room, Colby expressed regrets that his wife would not be present. He explained that she was visiting her family in the East and would return in a few weeks. After they went into the dining room they heard voices from the front room. 'Ah,' the major said. 'That must be Tom.'

A tall man with brown hair and a rugged, handsome look entered the room.

Major Colby introduced them. 'Matt Stone, Spider McCaw, this is Tom Kimball, my foreman. The men shook hands and seated themselves at the table.

'Tom's been having supper with us on a regular basis the last few weeks,' Colby said. 'Fact is, he asked Laura to be his wife.' Everyone turned toward Laura. 'But I don't think she's given him an answer yet.'

*

Matt found the evening with the Colby family to be a bit-tersweet experience. The news that Laura might marry Tom Kimball caught him off guard, and the intensity of his disappointment came as a surprise. But Matt liked the entire Colby family and he did not intend to let his disap-pointment ruin the evening. Though Colby's wife was away, a pleasant family atmosphere manifested itself over the celebration. Matt found great appeal in the closeness and sharing he found here. He wished his own childhood could have been similar, but tragedy had struck his family twice. When Matt was ten, his father had disappeared while away on business. Foul play was suspected but a body was never found. Matt gradually took over most of the duties on the small Kansas farm. Seven years later his mother came down with pneumonia, and Matt never forgot the agony of watching her slip into the death grip of the illness. Matt stayed with the farm for over a year but his heart was no longer in it. When an extended heatwave caused him to lose part of his crop, he sold out and drifted west. Three years later, he met Spider and the two became close friends.

As the evening progressed, Matt engaged in far-reach-ing discussions with his host and discovered what he had expected: Major Colby was not only a person of insight and integrity, he was exceedingly likeable. After supper, Matt spent considerable time with Katie. The bond formed with the young girl on the previous day strength-ened. After Katie finally went to bed, the two guests spoke at length with Colby, who expressed concern over recent events in Pine Valley and beyond. He indicated the outlaws were increasing in numbers and becoming far more aggressive. Many of the local ranchers expressed a heightened sense of alarm, and Colby expected another strike soon.

So far, all attempts to stop the marauders had failed. They just disappeared in the mountains without a trace.

CHAPTER 7

Major Colby rose early the next morning and had breakfast with Matt and Spider. On the previous evening, the
major had invited them to look over part of his range.
They set out immediately after their meal. The Box C
range covered much of Pine Valley and the adjacent
foothills. Two small creeks provided adequate water and
made the range ideally suited for cattle ranching. The
drought had reduced the amount of grass, but there were
still sufficient quantities available for the Box C herd.

It was just before noon when the three men stopped at
a high point along the upper edge of the valley. Colby
spoke as he dismounted. 'We'll rest the horses a spell
before heading back.' He walked to an overlook that provided a panoramic view of the valley with the Blue
Mountain range in the background. This was a favorite
vista for Colby. He had come here numerous times to con-
template his ranch and the natural beauty of the valley.
They stood in silence for a moment with each man viewing
the scenic valley in his own way. Colby thought of the many
years of toil spent on his ranch. He was gratified by his
accomplishments and he looked out over the valley with
pride.

After enjoying the view, Colby walked toward his horse
and then turned to look at the two men gazing across the

valley. Although Matt and Spider were quite different in appearance and temperament, Colby was sure of two things: they both had a solid streak of honesty, and they seemed very capable under extreme circumstances.

Colby looked at the taller of the two with admiration. He thought Matt was at least two inches over six feet, which contributed to his lean, rangy appearance. Matt had a full shock of light brown hair, almost sandy in colour. His face was well defined and set off by a strong jaw. The small scar over his right cheek did not detract from his overall handsome appearance. Colby's glance shifted to Spider, who was short, stocky, and obviously very strong for his size. Reports from the saloon attested to this fact. Spider's black hair never seemed to stay in place. There were early signs of hair loss, and it appeared this process might accelerate at any time. His face seemed to have a perpetual stubble, but his eyes stood above all else. They were dark and haunting. The intensity of the man could easily be seen in his face. During the previous evening Colby had listened to the two men talk of their friendship. It was obvious they had formed a loyal bond; the kind of friendship in which each would lay down his life to save the other. Colby thought many men went through life without ever experiencing such a relationship.

Colby had slept little the previous night. The recent increase in violence caused him great concern for his family and his ranch. The arrival of Matt and Spider had set his mind in motion. Colby contemplated a plan as he watched the two men.

Matt gazed out over the valley and was inspired by the rugged natural beauty of the region as he watched a hawk sail effortlessly across the sky. When he turned away from the edge, Colby stepped forward and said, 'I've been thinking about something all day that involves both of you.

I want you to come to work for me. I owe you as much for what you did for Katie, but I also know good men when I see them. I'll give you a solid increase over what Jarrod paid you. I know you may have ties back in Antelope, but I also know you'll like it here.' Colby glanced toward the valley, then looked directly at the two men. 'There's another reason I want you to work for me. I told you about the outlaws, so I'll tell you straight out. I need help.'

'The outlaws?' Matt asked.

'Yes, they're getting out of control. They strike quick and then go back into the hills. We just haven't been able to do much to stop them. This entire region is under attack from these gunmen and they're getting the best of us right now.'

'We followed those murderers up there,' Spider said, gazing off toward the mountains. 'There's hundreds of spots to hide up there. It's damn sure tough country to search.'

'It's cost us a lot of good men,' Colby replied. 'Every time we send men up there . . . some of them don't come back. People around here have started calling that mountain by a new name.'

'What name?' Matt asked.

'Death Mountain. It's that bad.'

'Do you know anything about this gang?' Spider asked. 'Where'd they come from?'

'The best we can figure is they came from Mosquito Creek. That's a rough mining town about eighty miles to the north. The gold ran out and the scum drifted down here. I guess they figured us for an easy mark and set up shop in the mountains. You can always find a bunch of them hanging out in the saloons in town. It's gotten so bad that good people are starting to leave.' Colby removed his hat and ran a hand through his silver hair, concern showed on his face. 'I need help and I know you two can take care of yourselves. Fuzzy told me about your scuffle in town. Matt, you're the first man around here to ever stand up to Jace Caldwell. A couple of others tried but it cost them their lives.'

'What about the sheriff?' Spider asked.

'Potter's a good man, but this thing is just too big for him. He's only got two deputies left and he probably needs a dozen for this job.'

Matt glanced toward the Blue Mountains. 'One thing's for sure. Two deputies aren't enough to roust that gang out of those mountains.'

'I know,' Colby replied. 'But that's not all. When something happens we simply can't prove who did it.'

Spider spoke up with anger in his voice. 'You've got to catch them red-handed and string them up on the spot.'

'The idea has some appeal,' Colby said, 'but we can't operate outside the law. If we catch any of them we'll turn them in for trial. The problem is that we can't find their hideout. They just disappear.'

'We may be able to help,' Matt said, 'but we need a little time to think on this. We'll let you know tomorrow.' The idea of working for Colby intrigued Matt, but he would not commit to anything before talking with his partner. They mounted and prepared to return to the ranch. As soon as he was in the saddle, Matt said, 'Major, there's one other thing we've got to consider.'

'What's that?'

'Jarrod let us run some steers on his range, and we could brand any calves that were sucking on our cows each spring. We've got about three hundred head under the Double S brand.'

Colby answered without hesitation. 'I normally wouldn't want to mix other brands in the valley, but because you saved Katie's life you're more than welcome to bring them over. Hell, I'll even add a few calves of mine to your bunch.'

They returned to the ranch in the early afternoon and saw Katie sitting atop the gate waiting for them. When they got close enough she yelled out, 'Hi, Daddy. Hello, Mr McCaw.' She held her arms out for Matt who swung his horse over, then helped her up behind him. After she was comfortable, Katie turned to her father. 'Daddy, Mr Kimball is waiting for you. He's very upset.'

Colby spurred his horse and rode toward the house where Tom Kimball could be seen waiting on the porch. Matt watched the two men as he approached the house. From Colby's reaction to Kimball, it was obvious the foreman was delivering disturbing news.

When Matt reached the house he saw Laura watching through the window, but she quickly disappeared when he looked up.

Katie leaned forward and whispered in his ear. 'I think she likes you, Mr Stone.' She giggled as Matt helped her down, then she disappeared into the house.

Spider had gone to the barn and was talking to two cowhands. Not wanting to intrude in Colby's business, Matt started toward the barn.

'Hold on, Matt,' Colby said, motioning for him to join them.

Matt approached the two men. 'Hello, Tom.'

'Howdy, Matt. I was just telling the major that we got hit pretty hard last night. The Mosquito Creek gang ran off a bunch of cattle from the east end.'

'That's not all,' Colby added. 'Tom said they also hit the bank in Clayton yesterday. That's about thirty miles west of here.' Major Colby began pacing back and forth, visibly concerned.

'Sounds like there's a helluva big pack of them,' Matt said, casting a sympathetic look toward Colby. 'They just hit our ranch, then strike yours, then hit a bank to the west.'

55

Colby stopped pacing and looked toward the mountains. 'The stakes have gone up and we need more men. This is going to turn into a damn war.'

'Major,' Tom said. 'It may not be that bad.'

'The hell it isn't,' Colby said, turning to his foreman. 'It's going to get a lot worse. Because of that I've asked Matt and his partner to work for us. They'll give us their answer in the morning. I also want you to hire two more men right away, and I don't want ordinary cowhands this time. I want good, honest men who can handle a gun. And I want them now.'

This was a new side of Major Colby, and Matt admired his resolve. The man's way of life was being threatened and he was stepping up to the challenge. 'Major, if we accept your offer I know two men that fit that description. They worked for Jarrod Kern and I know they'll want to leave if we do. They're honest and tough-nosed and I'll vouch for them.'

A look of optimism flashed through Colby's eyes. 'Now we're getting somewhere.'

At that very moment, Matt decided he wanted to accept Colby's offer – but he still had to talk it over with Spider.

That evening, Matt and Spider took supper with the Box C cowhands. They wanted to get a feel for the type of men they might work with. The roundup was finished, but most of the crew were still out on the range because protection of the herd was now their primary job. But the few that sat around the supper table were a good lot.

Matt especially liked Fuzzy Thurman, who he had met in town, and Punch Mitchell. Punch was two inches under six feet, stocky, and broad-shouldered. His hair was blond and he had small scars on his forehead and left ear. Punch did not have the usual background for a cowhand. He had a little college instruction, he had been a prize fighter for a few years, and most recently, he had been a deck hand on a freighting vessel.

Fuzzy Thurman was a typical cowboy. A little raw, but he was honest and hardworking. What remained of his dark hair poked out from under a hat that he never took off, except in the presence of women. It was said he even wore it to bed. His specialty was horses, and he was known to be the best trainer of cutting horses in the entire region.

After an enjoyable supper, Matt walked to the corral with Spider where they leaned on wooden rails and talked. It was immediately obvious they both wanted to accept Colby's offer, and they agreed to do so if conditions at the Kern ranch were stable. They did not expect any problems there, because they had left the ranch in the capable hands of Cliff Conner. They knew his loyalty and judgment were sound. The two men continued talking as they looked out over the ranch.

After a few minutes, Colby and his foreman came out of the house and walked toward them. When Colby was a few feet away, Matt said, 'Major, we're not gonna wait till morning. We're taking you up on that offer, but with one proviso.'

'Name it.'

'We left the ranch in good hands, but we want to make sure things are running smooth before we leave.'

'I expected as much. It's not a problem.'

'All right, you've got a deal.'

A wide smile crossed Colby's face. He extended his arm and vigorously shook hands with the two men. 'I'm delighted. How about that, Tom, we've added some muscle to our bunch.'

Kimball hesitated, then shook their hands. 'Glad to have you men with us.'

Matt looked back at Colby. 'We figure it'd be best if we left right away to get our cattle. I'm sure the other men I told you about will want to come back with us, and that will make our return trip easier.'

Colby rubbed his chin as his face took on a more serious look. 'I've been thinking on that. You'll have a tough time getting your cattle through the mountains. If that Mosquito Creek gang finds out you're coming through they'll be laying for you. I'm gonna send two of my men with you. I'd send more, but I'm short as it is.'

Matt pulled out a piece of rawhide and stuck it in the corner of his mouth. 'That'll give us six good men,' he said. 'We should be able to handle it.'

'Don't take any chances,' Colby replied.

'By the way,' Matt asked. 'What's the best route for driving cattle back to the Box C?'

'I'll send Fuzzy and Hawkins with you. Fuzzy knows the mountains better than anyone around.' Colby turned to his foreman. 'Tom, what do you think?'

'There are two logical routes. Fuzzy knows which one is best.'

Matt looked toward the mountains. 'All right, we'll leave in the morning.'

'I'll start on our gear,' Spider said, turning toward the barn.

Colby stepped closer to Matt and put a hand on his shoulder. 'Matt, be careful. That's a ruthless bunch up there. They'll kill a man just for the fun of it.'

CHAPTER 8

Matt and his three companions left for Antelope Valley at dawn the following morning. Shortly after their departure, Tom Kimball mounted his horse and set a course for Bear Mountain. The tall, handsome man was worried as he left the valley and entered the foothills. Recent events had not gone as he had expected, and he was becoming deeply entangled in a nightmare caused by his own poor judgement. His problems had begun seven months earlier with a simple poker game against a new arrival in town, a man named Fats Braddock from Mosquito Creek. Kimball had easily won that first poker game with Braddock, and he had won consistently over the next two weeks. Then his fortunes took a sudden change for the worse.

Fats Braddock had been cheating suckers out of money at poker for nearly twenty years, and Tom Kimball had been an easy mark. Braddock let Kimball win at first – then he pulled the string. It was all very well planned. Within two months, Kimball was heavily in debt to Braddock. He retraced the events over and over in his mind, but still could not understand how he had allowed himself to get in so deep. There was no possible way he could repay the debt from his monthly salary. Tom Kimball had fallen in love with Laura Colby before his debts began to rise. After asking Laura for her hand in marriage, he became increasingly obsessed that she would learn of his gambling problem and decline his proposal.

Deeply disturbed, Kimball had sought a way out of his predicament, and Fats Braddock was quick to oblige. It all seemed so easy – he would supply Braddock with information about local ranches and movements of the sheriff. In due course, his debt would be cancelled. Kimball felt he had to keep his dilemma secret. Laura must never find out. The Box C and others would lose a few steers but no one would be hurt. He would then be able to marry Laura and everything would fall into place. What Kimball did not know was that Braddock had shrewdly planned the whole thing from the beginning, and Fats was not about to let a good source of information go free.

It was late afternoon when Kimball wound his way along narrow trails and neared the outlaw hideout. He was a day late in reporting to Braddock, but the ranch guests had made it impossible for him to leave the previous day. Kimball was uneasy as he approached his destination. He always felt nervous in his meetings with Braddock – the man was ruthless.

Some men are born to be farmers, doctors, or tradesmen, and a few can be moulded into renowned artists or musicians. But Fats Braddock found his niche at cheating, stealing, and murder – and he was damn good at all three. Everyone who saw Braddock thought he was anything but an impressive-looking man. In fact, his appearance bordered somewhere between ugly and grotesque. He was obese, with an excessive girth that was often burdensome. What remained of his pitch black hair was stringy and unkempt. His round face always seemed oily. His dark, protruding eyes were set under thick eyelashes.

Despite this, Braddock was a formidable foe for any

man. His greatest asset was his mind and he knew it. His calculating intellect, along with an uncanny ability to judge men, were his true strengths. But there was something else about this fat, chain-smoking man that made him a dreaded enemy. Something vital had been left out of this man's psyche. Something was missing and it made him deadly – he had no concern for human life. Over the years he had ordered many men killed for little or no reason. Braddock simply did away with any obstacle that stood between him and his goals – and he did it without a second thought.

Braddock's last occupation was the owner of a sleazy saloon and brothel in Mosquito Creek. Speculation of a long life for the recent gold find in the area was unfounded, and Mosquito Creek died almost as fast as it had sprung up. Braddock was in business for such a short time that he was unable to recover his initial investment. He took a loss in the venture and was determined to reverse his fortunes at the expense of the people of Benbow and the surrounding area.

He had picked this region because of its proximity to Mosquito Creek, and because the remote territory was ideally suited for his clandestine activities. Plenty of easy targets were available in all directions, and superb conditions abounded for establishing long term hideouts. In fact, his location on the north-west side of Bear Mountain was the best hideout he had ever seen anywhere. Braddock liked the name the people of Benbow had recently bestowed on this huge profusion of rock – Death Mountain.

When Braddock had set up shop in Benbow, as a gambler, he had more lucrative goals in mind. He began by quietly gathering a large group of outlaws for his ventures and realized he needed a secure hideout.

Braddock's right-hand man, Jace Caldwell, had been

given the job of finding a potential stronghold, and he was the one who had found the unique location. During his search of the mountains, Caldwell had sought relief from a brief, but fierce thunderstorm. At the time the storm broke he had been riding along the bottom of a cliff and had sought shelter against the wall. As he had wove his way over large rocks he noticed a coyote running straight at the wall at high speed. The animal made no attempt to slow and ran straight into the heavy brush that lined the bottom of the cliff wall.

The coyote should have bounced off the wall and been seriously injured. Caldwell dismounted and immediately went to inspect the base of the cliff. He soon realized the mass of small rocks he was climbing over were mine tailings, now covered over by time. When he reached the top he dropped to his knees and poked his head into the spot where the coyote had disappeared. He found a series of deteriorating wooden planks spread across a black hole that was obviously the entrance to an old, long-forgotten mine. Caldwell moved a portion of the brush aside and yanked on the old boards. The wood had decayed to the point that only minimal pressure was required to loosen the planks. He crawled through the opening and entered the shaft.

While waiting for the storm to pass, he explored the mine and made a surprising discovery. The shaft ended just over a hundred feet inside the mountain. At that point, a wide fissure in the rock intersected the tunnel. The crack widened as one looked up, and Caldwell found easy access along the fracture to an upper level. To his amazement, he found a small enclosed basin within the high cliff walls. The basin was complete with a small pond created by snow run-off.

When Fats Braddock was brought to the site his devious intellect went into action. He found everything about the location to be perfect except the entrance. Braddock studied the tunnel for days before he struck on an ambitious, but shrewd strategy. He quickly despatched riders to town with a list of materials needed for his project. Three weeks later a hidden entrance had been devised, and access for horses from the inside of the tunnel to the basin was established. Most of the tailings were then hauled away. Removal of the small rocks uncovered medium-sized boulders that effectively impeded direct approach to the tunnel entrance.

The key elements to his project were brilliant. New shoring beams were placed in the weaker sections of the tunnel and on each side of the opening. A heavy wooden door, just wide enough to allow passage of a single horse was secured to the new beams. The work was performed with care so that the heavy natural brush remained intact. When the tailings had been removed, there was a drop of several feet to the large boulders below the entrance, which made access by horse impossible. Braddock sent his men two miles into the woods to fall a large tree. With considerable effort, a large plank was cut from the tree, then holes were drilled in one end of the thick timber and grooves were cut on one side. The plank was designed to allow passage by one horse at a time.

A team of horses hauled the plank to the shaft opening and it was pulled inside. The span was placed on an incline just inside the entrance. The plank could be easily pushed down because of the angle and a horse used to pull it back after use, similar to a drawbridge. Once inside the tunnel, the fissure acted as a natural stairway into the basin above. Horses made the climb with little difficulty. Inside the basin, two small buildings had been constructed, and a larger bunkhouse-type building was nearing completion. One of the finished buildings served as Braddock's sleeping quarters and office. The other building was used primarily as a kitchen.

Soon after setting up camp, Braddock had his men thoroughly search the entire area. Their inspection found that it was possible to scale the other side of the basin and exit on to the mountain itself. However, the climb would require considerable skill and was extremely dangerous. The men all agreed they would not use this route unless forced to. The inspection located a second exit. Halfway up the south wall, a narrow crack led directly into Rattlesnake Canyon, which ran adjacent to the basin. Passage through the gap was relatively easy on foot, but it was unsuitable for horses. Exit through Rattlesnake Canyon would only be used for emergencies, and then only in the winter when the large population of snakes were in deep underground dens.

Any attempt at passage through this canyon during other times of the year would bring instant terror to the trespasser and a good chance of death. Rattlesnake Canyon had received its name for good reason. Many locals said the narrow box canyon was home to more rattlers per square yard than anywhere else on earth. Stories were often told of unsuspecting miners being found with swollen bodies with as many as six different snake bites. Numerous skeletons of both men and animals were scattered through the area. The predominant inhabitant of the canyon was the diamondback, the largest of all rattlesnakes.

The diamondbacks in the canyon grew to seven feet in length, and were most active in the spring and summer. During the winter months, the snakes went into deep holes or cracks in the earth and rock for protection from the low temperatures. A single den often contained over a hundred snakes.

*

Fats Braddock sat at a rough, wooden plank that served as both a supper table and a desk. The room was hazy with smoke from his almost non-stop use of cigarettes. He had arrived the previous day to give orders for another raid, and to punish the three men who had kidnapped Katie Colby. They had made their play without orders or consent from Braddock, and he meant to deal with them in a harsh manner. However, the men had not returned to camp – they obviously anticipated what was in store for them. He also had expected to receive news from Tom Kimball, but Kimball had not shown. Fats Braddock was not a man to be kept waiting.

Jace Caldwell had just entered the room when he heard shouts from outside. Fats poured himself a whiskey and spoke to Caldwell. 'Jace, find out what that's all about. It'd better be Kimball.' Fats brought the glass to his lips and paused for a few seconds while he listened to the sounds from outside. Satisfied there was no cause for alarm, he drank the contents of the glass with the snap of his wrist.

A few minutes later, Tom Kimball entered the room followed by Caldwell. Braddock sat back in his chair and cast a harsh stare at the new arrival. 'You're late.'

'I couldn't help it,' Kimball said nervously.

'Why not?'

'The two men that brought the Colby girl back were invited to the ranch. I was expected to be there.'

The mention of the girl renewed Braddock's anger over the recent incident. 'Those idiots. What a fool thing to do. The fastest way to pull these ranchers together would be to kidnap a child, and that's exactly what they did.'

Kimball glanced at the table and reached for the bottle. 'I need a drink.'

Braddock nodded toward a dirty glass next to the whiskey. He watched the foreman pour a shot and wondered how such a strong-looking man could turn to jelly so suddenly. He grunted with satisfaction when he realized he had caused the change.

'I heard one of those men was Matt Stone. That right?'

'Yeah, him and a fellow named McCaw.'

Braddock crushed the end of his cigarette in a plate. 'I've heard of Stone,' he said, 'but not McCaw. Stone is supposed to be a heller with a gun. We'll find out in due time.'

Kimball poured another drink as he spoke. 'Colby offered them a job and they took him up. They're bringing two more men with them.'

'That's not good. What else?'

'They've got a small string of cattle over in Antelope. The major's letting them bring the steers into Pine Valley.'

Jace Caldwell had been quietly lurking in the corner but he suddenly seemed interested. He moved to the centre of the room. 'Boss, we can knock them off and get the cattle all in one swoop.' Jace raised his voice a level, 'I'll take Stone out myself.'

Over time, Braddock had learned how to handle Caldwell. 'He's yours,' he said. He turned his attention back to Kimball. 'Which way are they coming?'

'The Loop Trail. Not more than five or six men.'

Braddock rolled another cigarette as he listened. After his first deep puff, he said in a low tone, 'Handle it, Jace.'

Caldwell smiled as he walked toward the door, 'Sure, Boss. It'll be their last drive.'

CHAPTER 9

Laura Colby stood alone on the porch and gazed toward the mountains. The ranch yard she looked across was less active than usual today. Only her father, Katie, and two ranch hands were on site. Tom Kimball and the two guests had left three days before. Tom had told her he was going to check cattle and would return in three or four days. But something bothered Laura. She found herself thinking about Matt Stone and not Tom. She vividly remembered when she first saw Matt, when their eyes first met. Her heart seemed to stop for a moment. She thought she would never forget that first look – the experience had been like none she had ever known. Yet, she felt disturbed and angry. Everyone expected her to accept Tom's marriage proposal, and she thought she should not be thinking about another man. She tried to put Matt out of her mind and started to return to the house. Just as she turned, Katie came outside.

Katie looked at her sister with a knowing smile. 'Betcha can't wait till Matt gets back.'

'Katie—' She did not finish her sentence. This is ridiculous, she thought; even Katie can see through me. She turned away. 'Katie, I have no idea what you're talking about.'

'I saw the way you looked at Mr Stone. He's very nice,

isn't he?'

'Mr Stone and Mr McCaw are both nice,' Laura said, 'but I don't want to hear you saying foolish things anymore.' With that, she entered the house and went into the kitchen. Her thoughts turned to Tom Kimball. For the second time in the past week she thought about Tom's recent behaviour. He seemed strange lately. At times he was distant and preoccupied – something was not right.

Matt, Spider, and the two Box C hands reached the Kern ranch without incident, and they immediately set about the task at hand. If it had not been for the recently completed roundup, Matt Stone and Spider McCaw would have found only a small portion of the cattle marked with their Double S brand. Because the roundup was over, their timing was fortunate. In the short time allotted they were able to locate two hundred and twenty of the estimated three hundred head they owned. The others would be held for future delivery as they were found.

As Matt suspected, both Boyd Cooper and Bill Hollis chose to accompany them and join Colby's Box C. None of the men was particularly anxious to leave the Kern ranch but they did not want to work for Jarrod's brother, who was scheduled to arrive in three days. Matt and Paul Kern had not gotten along since their very first meeting. There was a general consensus among the older hands that Paul was not the equal of Jarrod and never would be.

Cliff Conner had hired several new hands and the ranch was running smoothly. After a lengthy discussion, it was decided there was no reason to delay the trip back to the Box C. Early the next morning, the men drove the cattle out of holding pens and left the Kern ranch. Travel across the valley was easy, but each man knew things might be very different once they reached the mountains. Fuzzy Thurman had told Matt there were two suitable routes for driving cattle to Pine Valley: one was shorter and easier, but it would also be the most dangerous. It was common knowledge to the people of Pine Valley that the trail was watched by outlaws. For this reason, Fuzzy recommended the other route, which was known as the Loop Trail.

After hearing details of both routes, Matt agreed with Fuzzy and they set a course for the Loop. They followed familiar terrain for the first three days until they were well into the mountains. The following morning, Fuzzy sent Jim Hawkins to ride point and lead the way to the Loop. They turned on to a narrow trail that led through thick pines and followed it for most of the day. It was late afternoon when the path widened and came to a small meadow. Fuzzy pulled up next to Matt. 'The Loop starts at the far end of this meadow, but we should make camp here tonight because we won't come to another likely spot today.'

'How long till we reach Pine Valley?'

'Two days. The Loop comes out at the end of the valley. It's another half day from there to the house.'

'All right,' Matt said as he scanned the meadow. He turned back to Fuzzy. 'I'm going to scout the area and make sure we're alone. I'll be back in about an hour.' Matt was uneasy as he rode into the timber. He felt as if they were being watched. He was so concerned that he made a larger circle than he had intended, carefully looking for tracks or any other signs of recent activity. After a search of over an hour, he was relieved to find the only fresh markings belonged to animals. The few horse tracks he came across were several days old.

Until now, two men had been on guard during the night, but because of Matt's concern he changed the number to three from now until they were safely into Pine Valley. Guard duty would be rotated to ensure each man got nearly the same amount of sleep. The next morning, the small herd had to be prodded to leave the meadow, but once they got on to the trail they made reasonable progress. At mid-morning, they left the heavy timber and entered much rougher country. They came to a series of rock gorges and travel slowed considerably. Matt sent a man to scout each gorge before they entered.

In late afternoon, they left the rougher country and again entered timber. After another hour, they came to a section of the trail with a steep tree-covered slope on their right. They were moving below the slope when shots rang out. Matt saw Hawkins go down with the first heavy barrage. It looked as though he took several hits at once. From the way Hawkins fell, Matt thought he was surely dead.

Heavy firing came from all along the top of the ridge to their right. Chaos descended on the trail below. The narrowing of the pathway at this point had caused the cattle and riders to be strung out over a considerable distance. The eruption of gunfire sent the cattle bolting in panic. They fled in all directions – bawling loudly as they ran.

Matt was fortunate to be on the side opposite the steep slope. Heavy, wicked gunfire continued to pour down on the trail from the top of the slope. Trees obscured the upper part of the ridge from his position, and he was able to gain cover with only a few shots coming his direction. He tied his horse to a tree behind large rocks and pulled his rifle from the boot. Matt was immediately concerned for his companions and tried to locate them as he peered over the rocks. He saw Fuzzy crouched behind a tree some thirty yards away, but he could see no one else. A considerable number of cattle could be seen running recklessly among the trees as gun shots continued to ring out from all directions. The heavy shooting in the narrow confines had confused and frightened the cattle into a terrible panic. Unable to find a route to freedom, most of the steers ran through whatever open area they could find. They frequently crashed into one another and many went down only to be trampled by their own kind. Visibility became poor as heavy dust and gun smoke filtered thickly through the trees. It was quickly becoming an untenable position.

Matt attempted to return the fire but his targets were obscured by trees. He continued to worry about the others and realized that if he were to help his friends he would have to move up the trail. His safety would be greatly jeopardized, but instinct drove him to make the move. Matt rose from behind the rocks and muttered to himself, 'Dammit! Somebody knew we were coming through here.'

Matt ran to his horse and opened his saddlebags. He obtained cartridges for both weapons and stuffed as many into his trousers as possible. He then shoved rifle shells into his vest pocket. After making sure the gunfire still came only from the opposite slope, Matt began to move through the trees on his side of the trail, staying high enough to avoid detection from the opposite ridge. He shortly came to a point above Fuzzy Thurman and yelled down. 'Fuzzy!' He waited. There was no response and Matt realized his voice could not penetrate the deafening roar of gunfire. He yelled louder.

Fuzzy jerked his head around and searched in the direction of the voice.

Matt waved and yelled, 'There're too many of them. Spread the word to pull out to whoever you can find. I'm going to work up the bottom of the slope and try get up on their flank. I'll give cover fire from there.' Matt heard Fuzzy yelling something about it being too dangerous, but he was determined to do something to reduce the heavy fire that rang down upon his companions. Fuzzy was still yelling at Matt as he made his way along the slope. He ignored the shouts and ran along the hill, keeping to whatever cover was available. When the gunfire grew more distant, he turned and went straight down to the trail and crossed to the other side.

The opposite slope was very steep and Matt broke into a sweat as he climbed toward the top of the ridge. He stopped often to check on the gunfire and to maintain his distance from the ambushers. To his relief, the gunmen had apparently made no attempt to flank his companions from this direction. Matt reached the top of the ridge and searched for a higher location that would offer a vantage point, but still provide good protection. There appeared to be a good spot on a ridge just behind the one he was on. If he could get to it he would have a superior position, but he worried if he could afford the time and the risk. Although fatigued from the climb, he made a dash down the far side of the slope and began to run up the parallel ridge that ran behind the first. His lungs began to sting as he scrambled up the slope and he soon came to an open area. If they saw him now he would make an easy target. The gunmen were evidently too intent on spraying bullets on the trail below and they did not watch their flank or the slope to their rear.

Breathing heavily, and in a full sweat, Matt dived behind cover atop the second ridge. He pulled out his revolver and laid it on a rock in front of him; then he placed a handful of rifle shells on the rock. When he rose to seek his target he was astonished at the large number of gunmen he could see firing from the top of the other ridge. Matt knew someone wanted him dead – very dead.

He scanned the area again, then raised his rifle and began to fire shots in rapid succession. One gunmen fell, then another. A third yelled when he was hit in the arm. A mad scramble for cover occurred along the ridge below. This was exactly what Matt wanted. If he could ease the firing pressure from the trail below, his friends might have a chance to escape. The outlaws located his position and sent a barrage of gunfire toward him, but Matt had expected this and dropped behind the rocks. Dozens of bullets flew in his direction as he crouched behind his cover. With that many guns, it would be foolhardy to expose himself for more than a split second. If they realized he was alone he also had to worry about them rushing his position. Nonetheless, he had to keep up the pressure – and right now.

Matt moved a few feet to his right, then rose up firing. After a few seconds, he moved as far as possible in the opposite direction and did the same. Although his shots were rapid, his aim was still good and the gunmen were paying a high price. But because of the sheer number of attackers, Matt knew he could not stay in his position long, but he was determined to help his friends escape.

CHAPTER 10

When Matt dropped to reload he heard a momentary cessation of gunfire from the opposite ridge. He took this as a sign the outlaws might be changing tactics. By now, the gunmen must have realized only one or two men were firing at them. They would soon try to take him out, and Matt knew they could easily do so with their overpowering numbers. He had to move.

Any attempt to go back in the direction he had come would provide an easy target on open ground, and he would be quickly cut down. Matt looked to his rear and found only a ragged cliff, but he thought he could follow the ridge he was on and hope for a way out. He might even be able to work his way back to his horse. But he suddenly realized that would not work – he would have to abandon his horse. They would obviously begin searching the trail and find the animal. His only chance was to get away fast.

He reloaded and took one more look over the rocks. There was movement along the slope and several men were coming in his direction. Matt fired several shots and then retrieved his revolver from the rock. He holstered the pistol and began running down the narrow ridge. He was temporarily safe from the gunmen while he moved in the opposite direction. In fact, he suddenly realized that he heard no gunfire at all. He took this as a sign his companions might have gotten away. Or the opposite could be true – they might already be dead. He reached the bottom and felt anything but relief as he looked out over a small, rock strewn plain. There were a few scattered clumps of trees wherever they could get a foothold in the rocks, but little else. This side of the ridge was decidedly different from the other. He thought he would surely die on this barren, rock-strewn plain.

There was little time now and he had to make a decision, but whatever choice he made Matt knew his chances were poor. He could swing around the two ridges and go back to the trail, but a large open stretch had to be crossed and the area was undoubtedly being searched at this very moment. He looked across the plain and saw a series of small hills lined with pine trees. Steep cliffs behind the trees eventually gave way to a rugged mountain slope. He could hide there, but there was no safe way across the flat ground. He glanced around to make sure he had not overlooked anything, and then made his decision. With rifle in hand, Matt began to run across the rock strewn plain, fully aware that he had one chance – he had to get safely across the stretch of red rock to the first clump of trees without being seen. He ran past several small crannies that would afford hiding from a distant observer, but he would easily be spotted by any horsemen that came near.

He kept running.

He was halfway to the first trees before he glanced back. He did not see any riders from the direction of the trail, but he did see men on top of the ridge – and they saw him. It would only be a short time before the gunmen rode out to shoot him down like an animal. Matt's sighting of the men stirred a new wave of stamina. Although he was beginning to fatigue he managed to increase his pace slightly. Cartridges in his vest thumped against his chest with each stride, the rifle suddenly seemed to be twice its original weight, and sweat poured from his forehead and ran into his eyes. Matt's legs began to feel as if they were made of lead instead of bone, muscle, and blood.

Still he pounded on.

He started to look back but was afraid he would lose his balance and fall. He had no energy left for such manoeuvres. He neared a small stand of trees and heard the first rifle shots. His original hope had been to reach the trees before being seen, but the outlaws had seen him and they were now bearing down on him on horseback. Matt's mind raced as he came to the first tree. A bullet crashed into the thick bark near his head as he rushed by. He knew he could force a temporary standoff from the trees, but he would not be able to hold them off for long. He had to keep running.

Hoping they would think he would stop in the first group of trees, Matt continued on with the same stride. His only hope was to reach the tree-covered ridges beyond, but his body was now sending out harsh signals of fatigue and pain. The sting in his lungs had increased to a sharp burn, and his legs did not respond to his wishes. His mind was yelling at his legs to continue, or even quicken their pace, but there was no response. Suffering from exhaustion, Matt began to slow with each stride. He came out of the rear side of the trees and looked toward the ridge ahead. It was only two hundred yards now. There was no gunfire from behind – he might make it. He plodded along for over a hundred yards and then looked over his shoulder just as horsemen came around the edge of the trees. Matt turned his head forward and his right boot grazed a rock and he crashed to the ground. His Winchester skidded across the rocks. He scrambled on his hands and knees, retrieved the rifle, and turned toward the gunmen. Three riders were now charging straight at him. Puffs of smoke discharged from their guns and bullets hit all around him.

He took a firing position and tried to aim but his body shook from the extreme effort during the run, and the sweat pouring into his eyes obscured his vision. Still, he had to fire. Shaking, his first shot carried wide of its mark. His second shot struck a horse and sent the animal sprawling; the rider crashed heavily into the rocks, striking his head on a large stone. The other riders continued toward him. He had to take better aim. Matt had only seconds now and again sighted his rifle. A bullet ricocheted off a rock next to him as his gun roared once more.

The lead rider took a bullet in the neck and instantly fell from his saddle. The horse veered to one side and continued running, his ears pinned back. When the last rider saw the odds had turned even, he bolted his horse to the side and turned back toward the trees. Matt got up and ran in an uneven gait toward the knoll directly in front of him. When he started up the incline he looked back and saw six more gunmen coming around the far edge of the clump of trees. They reached the lone rider and stopped briefly; then the entire group rode straight toward Matt.

The first ridge was not high, only about thirty feet. Matt dived over the top, then turned and placed his rifle on the dirt for stability. He was still shaking. Without picking individual targets, he fired rapidly into the middle of the pack. The riders suddenly split off in two groups, as if prearranged, and kept at a safe distance as they raced toward the ridge on either side of his position. This was exactly what Matt wanted; this would buy him a few precious minutes. He turned and scurried up the next slope, falling twice only to recover and continue on. Sweat and dust covered his body as he scrambled and clawed his way higher. He was into the trees now and pushed ahead recklessly, pleading with his legs to keep moving. He had to reach a position where he could not be pursued on horse-back. That was his only chance.

He crossed the top of the second ridge and ran blindly through the trees toward the cliff. His lungs burned and he was sucking air in huge, rapid gulps. He tripped on exposed roots and fell face down. He raised his head and spat out a mouthful of dirt. Still, he rose again.

Matt looked at the cliff in front of him and his heart sank. The walls appeared to be very jagged when he had observed them from a distance, but he saw nothing that would allow him to climb safely. He could only hope there was a gap in the wall that he could not see. He came out of the scattered trees and stood before the wall. There was no access here but, as he glanced to his right, there were numerous large cracks in the uneven cliff. But he also knew there were now gunmen somewhere on that side.

With no other options, Matt ran toward the cracks as fast as his tired legs allowed. He heard shouts in the distance as he began to climb the coarse rock, but he did not look back. He had to get high on the wall to an area that would provide cover and be a good defensive position. If there was no other way up, he might gain a temporary standoff. His chest ached as he neared a pocket of rock two thirds of the way up the wall. A sudden barrage of gun-shots sounded from below and bullets bit into the rocks around him. Just as Matt dived into the protected area, a bullet struck his right boot, tearing off the heel.

Instead of immediately returning fire, Matt sat with his back against a large rock and gulped air. He had never been this physically exhausted in his entire life. Every thread of his clothing was soaked with sweat. It took an unbelievable effort to reach this spot and he was thankful for his stamina. After catching his breath, he exchanged rifle shots with the outlaws until the sun went down. He was able to keep them on the defensive because of his excellent location. Anyone who tried to climb toward him during daylight hours was at a severe disadvantage. No one tried. But he knew it would be different after dark. When he was not watching below, Matt studied the wall above. He had to climb higher as soon as it became dark. Because of the difficulty of climbing at night, he studied the rock wall over and over. When the sun went down, his intended route was precisely etched in his mind.

After firing several shots to keep the gunmen on edge, Matt quietly worked his way toward the top. The climb was actually easier than he had expected because he was somewhat renewed from his rest. Matt reached the top and found several small boulders perched on the edge of the cliff. With the help of a small limb he managed to push three of the large rocks over the edge, hoping they would break other rocks loose, causing confusion below, if not injury.

He then turned and descended about three hundred feet before reaching heavy timber. He headed west with a combination of slow running and fast walking. If he kept this up for a few hours, he thought, his chances would increase dramatically. After a short distance, fatigue again became his enemy and he had to stop for longer than he wanted. Whenever Matt found enough rocks, he changed course and crossed them, hoping to disguise his route by keeping off the ground as much as possible. At one point, he found a series of large boulders and was able to travel a considerable distance by jumping from one boulder to the next.

Though his body ached with exhaustion, he plodded on. It was near midnight before Matt finally sought shelter. Though in need of water, he crawled beneath a small overhang in a rock outcropping and fell asleep within minutes.

CHAPTER 11

The morning after the ambush, Spider McCaw watched the sun rise as he drank coffee. Besides himself, three of the six men who had begun the trip to Pine Valley were present. Hawkins was dead and Matt was missing. Spider finished breakfast and waited while Fuzzy tended the bullet wound in Bill Hollis' leg. Others would have been killed if Matt had not been able to divert the heavy gunfire that had rained down on the trail. Spider knew what his friend had done, and he was more worried about Matt than he had ever been. Spider knew there was a good chance Matt had sacrificed himself to save the others. He felt deep concern as he gazed out over the mountains.

Because of Hollis' leg, it had already been decided that Fuzzy Thurman and Boyd Cooper would leave with the wounded man and head directly for the Box C. Although Spider knew Matt would not wish it, he meant to stay behind and search for his friend. Even if Matt was alive, Spider thought the chances of finding him were poor, but he had to try. There were several obstacles in his way, including limited knowledge of the terrain, but his biggest problem was the large number of outlaws who were probably still in the area. Spider walked to the small fire and covered it with dirt.

Fuzzy glanced at him. 'I still think you should ride in

with us. Hell, Matt may be on his way to the ranch right now. If not, we could get supplies and a few more men and put out a search party. We're not far away so it won't take long.'

Spider finished with the fire and looked toward the mountains. 'I'll see if I can pick up any sign of him. If I do, I'll stick with it. If not, I'll come in and we'll do it your way.'

'All right, but watch out for those gunmen. Those sons of bitches are probably all over that whole area.'

'I know.' Spider walked toward the wounded man. 'It's awful hard to kill an old hog like you, Bill. You're gonna be just fine.'

'Thanks, Spider. I'll be all right . . . but you watch yourself.'

A few minutes later, Fuzzy and Cooper helped Hollis on to his horse. The wound was not too severe, but there had been a substantial loss of blood, which was causing occasional dizzy spells.

Before they left for the Box C, Spider had the men give him information about the surrounding area. The men then left for the ranch. Spider watched for a while, then mounted and rode off in the other direction to search for Matt. He hoped to find his friend, but he knew there was a good chance Matt had been killed.

For the last two days, both Laura and Katie Colby could often be seen looking across the valley toward the mountains. Laura's glances were less obvious than those of her sister, but she looked at least as often. She was genuinely concerned for everyone's safety, but she was also looking for Matt, and each time Laura caught herself thinking of him she felt confused by a strange mixture of feelings. Tom Kimball had come back a few days earlier, but he had remained for only a short time before leaving again. Laura noticed he was coming and going more than usual recently, but what really concerned her was his changing behaviour.

It was late afternoon when Laura saw the horses.

Katie came running toward the house. 'They're back! They're back.'

As the horses drew closer, Laura counted only three. Four had left the ranch and one or two more from the Kern ranch were supposed to have joined them. Some of them didn't make it back. Concern crept across Laura's face as she went to the edge of the porch to meet Katie.

'Laura . . . Laura. They're home.'

'Calm down, Katie,' she answered, putting one arm around her sister. 'There are only three of them.'

Katie had obviously not thought to count the horses. She spun around and peered intently at the approaching riders. When the men were close enough to see, Laura realized that both Matt and Spider were missing. Her heart sank.

Major Colby heard Katie's shouts and came out of the barn to investigate. He saw the riders and hurried to meet them. He could tell by the way Hollis was riding that he was hurt, though Colby was on the wrong side to see the bloody leg.

Fuzzy Thurman pulled to a stop. 'They ambushed us on the Loop. Bill took a bullet in his right leg and he's lost a lot of blood.'

Colby motioned toward the house. 'Let's get him inside.' He walked toward the house and called to one of his men near the barn, 'Martin, get into Benbow and get the doc. Tell him we've got a gunshot wound out here and tell him to hurry.'

Fuzzy dismounted and spoke solemnly to the major. 'Hawk's dead.'

Colby expected bad news because there were only three

riders, but it still hit hard. Hawkins had been with him for a long time. 'Damn,' he said in a distraught tone. Sadness swept over him and it was a long moment before he spoke. 'Let's take care of Bill. Then I want to hear everything.'

Laura feared that Matt and Spider had also been shot, but her instincts sent her into the kitchen for supplies to nurse Hollis. She obtained water and dressing material and then went into the bedroom where the wounded man had been taken. She began working on the leg and listened intently as the men discussed the ambush.

After Colby made sure Hollis was comfortable, he spoke to Fuzzy. 'What about the others?'

'Spider's out looking for Matt, but we figure they must've shot him.'

The scissors fell from Laura's hands.

'How'd it happen?' Colby asked.

'They knew we were going to be there. No doubt about it. They had over twenty guns on top of a ridge waiting for us. They laid into us and we couldn't even see them. Hawkins took the first bullet; then all hell broke loose.'

'Was it the Mosquito Creek bunch?'

'We couldn't see them, but I'm sure of it. Who else has that many men?'

After hearing details of the ambush, Colby expressed concern over how the outlaws received their information. But they all knew one thing for sure – Fuzzy was right. There would not be that many men waiting on the trail by chance. Somebody told them.

Laura tended Bill Hollis until Doc Hansen arrived that evening, then she assisted the doctor when he cleaned and dressed the wound. After Hollis was resting comfortably, Laura went to check on Katie. She knew her younger sister had developed a friendship with Matt and was concerned for her. But it was not until she saw Katie that she realized just how strong the bond was.

Katie's face was puffy and her eyes were red. She had obviously been crying during the evening. She was seated with her father who was speaking to her in a comforting voice. Colby looked up as Laura entered the room. 'It seems Katie has made up her mind that Matt's been shot. I've told her no one knows for sure and he's probably just lost. Don't you think so, Laura?'

Laura knew her father was trying to ease Katie's pain and she wanted to help, but her first attempt at words failed. Laura tried again and spoke softly. 'I'm sure he's all right, Katie. He'll be back. . . . Just wait and see.'

'He's probably sitting by a warm fire right now,' her father added. 'He's a smart fellow and a fine man. Isn't that right, Laura?'

Laura's gaze dropped to her lap. 'Y-yes, he is.'

The following morning, Major Colby rose early to check on Hollis. Although the wounded man was weak, he had no temperature and it appeared he might avoid infection. After his talk with Hollis, Colby went into the kitchen where his cook, Marie, was busy preparing dough for the morning biscuits. He poured coffee, then he headed toward the bunkhouse. When he was halfway across the yard, Fuzzy Thurman and Boyd Cooper came outside.

The very nature of ranch work required the men to rise early. They all accepted it as part of their job, but their demeanour varied considerably. Many were quiet and grumpy before breakfast, but an amazing transformation usually occurred after food and coffee. Fuzzy Thurman was different. Rain or shine, he rose in a cheerful mood. But this morning he was not smiling, and it was easy for the major to guess why. The lives of two Box C men were in jeopardy, and Fuzzy was more than a little protective of his own. Fuzzy brushed the top of his hat as Colby approached. He put on his hat and spoke to Colby, 'Mornin', Boss. Me and Coop was just talking about how long we should wait for Spider. What do you think?'

Colby had already given the matter much thought. 'Spider said he was going to come straight in if he didn't find any sign. Right?'

'That's what he said.'

'We'll give him till tomorrow noon, then we'll send out a search party.' The men talked at length about their plans for the next day. Details about who would go and how long to continue the search were agreed on.

Routine ranch matters occupied most of Colby's day, but he occasionally looked toward the mountains in hope of seeing two riders in the distance. Because of recent events, Colby would not let his daughters have their usual freedom to roam the valley. However, they did exert enough pressure on their father to gain permission to ride a short distance away from the house. But he made them promise to stay together and remain within sight.

The day passed with only one rider coming to the ranch. Doc Hansen came across the valley in mid-afternoon to check on Hollis' condition. He was met by two young ladies on horseback who eagerly rode toward him. But Doc was somewhat confused by their obvious disappointment when they recognized him. He knew his womanizing days were long over, but such a greeting was disheartening nonetheless. After a sigh, he spoke under his breath. 'Women weren't meant to be understood.'

The long day passed without the return of the two men. At mid-morning of the next day, Colby gave orders for the selected men to prepare their gear and be ready to ride before noon. Not wanting to leave the ranch unprotected, he limited the party to five men. He also gave them explicit instructions on how long to continue the search. He could not afford to have the men gone too long. Colby had to consider the safety of his daughters and of the entire ranch. He also knew Matt Stone and Spider McCaw were extremely capable individuals.

Just before noon, the search party left the ranch and rode toward the mountains. Laura and Katie rode with them as far as their father would allow. After the men were out of sight, the two sisters talked as they rode. From time to time, each would look out across the valley but neither saw any sign of the hoped-for riders.

CHAPTER 12

Matt awoke to the sound of horses. Startled, he scrambled away from the overhang and crawled behind a large boulder. He saw four riders two hundred feet to his left. By their manner he knew they were searching for him, but they did not appear to be following any particular tracks. The four men must have been given instructions to scour the countryside in an attempt to find the wanted man. They stopped twice, scanned the area, and then moved slowly toward the north.

With the sun well up in the eastern sky, Matt realized he had slept longer than he intended. Fatigue had obviously won out over desire. When he stood, pain shot through both of his legs. The intensity of the soreness caused him to lean against the rock and groan under his breath. During the vigorous running the previous day, he had strained muscles in both legs. He moved his legs up and down to loosen the muscles. Though sore, his legs gradually felt better and he thought walking would reduce the pain further. Matt quietly made his way through the trees. He moved slowly at first but gradually picked up his pace. After an hour he felt he was safely away from the four riders but he remained alert.

After another hour, his intense thirst demanded his attention. Matt expected to find small creeks among the pine trees, but the recent drought had caused many to dry up. He passed several small creek beds that contained little more than sand and rock. If he was unable to find water in a few hours he would try digging in one of the dry creek beds. If that failed, he would obtain fluids by eating plants and roots.

Matt continued to walk at a consistent pace for several hours. He headed west, following the sun. He thought this would bring him out somewhere in Pine Valley, though he had no idea where. Several times he spotted small game, but decided not to risk a shot as there was a strong chance the noise would carry to the wrong ears. He decided he would risk a shot only when he became desperate. He stopped occasionally to rest and search for water, but he was determined to maintain a steady pace as long as possible. In late afternoon, he had still not located water and he began to dig for edible roots. He searched for over two hours, digging with his hands at any likely vegetation. He chewed and sucked on the roots and managed to obtain some nutrition. After his hands began to bleed he stopped his search and pressed on. That night, he crawled behind a fallen tree and lay on his back. His thirst was so bad that he decided to consider risking a shot at small game the next day. He had to get fluids into his body.

The next morning he again headed west. He travelled for three hours and thought he heard running water. He angled toward the noise and, after a few minutes, came to a small creek about four feet wide. He looked about for a moment, then lay down and drank from the stream. The water was clear and cold and barely deep enough for him to emerge his entire head, which he did. Matt rested and drank more water as he considered his route to Pine Valley. The creek ran toward the west and there was a fair chance it met other streams and eventually reached the valley. When he and Spider rode across the Box C Ranch, they came to one creek and Colby told him of another at the far end of the valley. The one he had seen came out of the mountains to the east of the Pine Valley. This might be that same stream.

Matt did not know how much progress he made during the morning, but knew he had not gone too far due to excessive thirst. He checked the direction of the sun and decided to take a chance on the stream. There were two good reasons for following the water; the creek would take him to a lower elevation, and he would have constant access to drinking water. If the waterway changed course he could always change his plans and continue west.

Considerably refreshed from his rest, and with his thirst quenched, Matt resumed his journey. The stream he followed wound its way down the mountainside in snakelike fashion. There was no trail alongside the water, but travel was relatively easy. Just before dusk, he found a suitable spot to spend the night. The location was some fifty yards from the creek and offered the protection of rocks and trees. He was hungry, sore, and weary when he lay down, but sleep offered quick respite from his burdens.

Matt awoke at dawn and listened for a time before moving. He made his way to the stream and inspected the area carefully, but found no sign that anyone had passed by. Satisfied, he drank deeply but the gnawing hunger in his gut would not be satisfied by water alone. He decided if he could travel at least half a day without any sign of the outlaws it would be safe to shoot wild game. As the day wore on, Matt was pleased the creek continued in an uneven, but constant, journey toward the west. When another smaller waterway joined the one he followed, he became more optimistic that he was on the creek that ran into Pine Valley. The stream now contained just the right amount of water.

In mid-afternoon, Matt came out of heavy pines and

entered an area of scattered trees and heavy brush. There were numerous rabbits in the thick bushes and he decided to use his rifle. He took aim and downed a rabbit with one shot; then he carried the animal for an hour before stopping. He searched his pocket vest and found three matches. Dry grass and brush were plentiful and starting a fire would be easy. His pocket knife was not ideal for skinning the rabbit, but to a hungry man it looked like a Bowie knife. Matt ate and rested for a time and nearly dozed off. He immediately got to his feet and resumed his journey. He could not afford to rest – he had to keep going.

He walked a short distance and came to a small valley. Because it was nearly dark, he decided to camp among the trees above the valley. It was important to avoid being caught by horsemen in an open area. He inspected the terrain and found a suitable location. The stream meandered down the valley and disappeared around a bend directly toward the setting sun. Because the stream had moved so consistently westward, Matt was nearly positive the water would soon flow into Pine Valley.

He scouted the area briefly and then settled down to watch the last of the sun disappear in the western sky. He considered his circumstances and made plans for tomorrow. A few minutes later he fell asleep. The night was uneventful and Matt slept well. He rose with the sun, ate the rest of the rabbit, and went down to the stream for water. He then climbed back up the ridge and began to work his way along the northern slope not far from where he had camped. He meant to avoid the small valley during the day by staying on the ridge and continuing parallel with the course of the stream.

The water picked up speed and tumbled into a narrow gorge. After walking only two hours, Matt stood above the canyon and saw a large valley to the west. It had to be Pine Valley and he thought he could reach it in three hours. He moved carefully until he reached a small ridge at the edge of the valley. He recognized the area and was gratified the creek he followed was the one that ran near the ranch house. He estimated he could reach the house before day's end, but he would be exposed in the open for much of the time. He might be seen by outlaws, but it was also possible that he could meet Box C riders at any time.

The first two miles into the valley, Matt continually turned and checked his backside. Every step thereafter eased his concern but he still looked back regularly. It was late afternoon when Matt thought he saw the vague outline of the ranch complex. He walked a little farther until he saw two small specks in the distance. Matt picked up his pace and squinted. The specks grew larger and he could make out two riders.

When he got closer, one of the horses suddenly went into a gallop in his direction. As the rider came nearer, Matt recognized the nine-year-old girl he had quickly grown to love. It was Katie. Matt stopped and watched her ride toward him. She pulled up in front of him and shouted. 'You're safe! You're safe!' Katie dismounted and ran to Matt.

He bent down and hugged her.

While he held Katie, Laura pulled to a stop a few yards away. Matt saw relief etched across her face as their gazes met.

CHAPTER 13

Fats Braddock rode along a narrow trail toward his mountain hideout. As usual, several gunmen came along for his protection. Although no one was aware of his iron-fisted control over the Mosquito Creek outlaws, he always travelled in a cautious manner. He usually had at least three men along as guards, and it was always the same: two rode in front of him and one to his rear.

On this particular trip Braddock was more than upset – he was positively surly. The farther he went up the mountain the madder he became. Some of the men from the ambush had reported to him at the saloon and tried to explain what had happened. But only one fact stood out in Braddock's mind – his much larger force had lost several men against only one loss for the smaller group they attacked. But that was not all; most of the cattle were still running loose in the mountains.

Matt Stone had single-handedly killed several of his toughest gunfighters in a matter of days. Braddock knew the man was dangerous and would cause more problems in the future. He began to worry more about this one man than all of the lawmen in Benbow and the surrounding towns put together. Stone would have to be killed – and soon! Braddock would usually let Jace Caldwell handle this type of job, but the big gunman had been in charge of the failed ambush. Braddock went over the various options for getting rid of Matt Stone as he followed the trail.

It was dark when he reached the rock-covered ground in front of the hidden tunnel. Although the shaft entrance was extremely well concealed, Braddock had standing orders for everyone to enter and leave under cover of darkness whenever possible. Riders were also told to guide their horses over the rock slabs until they reached the area of heavy cattle tracks. Such efforts insured that no could follow horse tracks to the hidden entrance. Braddock went through the tunnel, entered the basin, and found the hideout to be sparsely occupied. A few of his men were in town to drink and gamble, while another group was driving a small herd of stolen cattle to his buyer.

Because of his excessive bulk, it always took a considerable effort for Braddock to mount and dismount the large horse he rode. When he finally stepped down on to a bench, the horse seemed relieved to be free of its heavy burden. Some thought it was an amusing sight to see the big man struggle with a seemingly simple task, but no one ever said a word. The last man that had laughed at his horsemanship was dead. Everyone who had seen the incident would never forget it. Braddock had walked over to the man who had laughed and shot him in the stomach. No warning, nothing. Braddock had simply pulled out a short-barrelled revolver and shot the man three times. No one had dared laugh at him since.

Before entering his shack, Fats called to one of his men. 'Is Jace here?'

'Yeah, he's in the bunkhouse.'

'Tell him to get his butt over here.' Braddock entered the small room and sat at the rough table. He rolled a cigarette and then poured a small glass of whiskey. He was drawing heavily on the cigarette when Caldwell entered the shack. Braddock studied the gunman for a few seconds before speaking. 'What's wrong with you, Jace? You can't even handle a simple damn ambush?'

'They got lucky,' Caldwell replied, obviously not anxious to talk about the incident.

'I don't think it was luck, Jace. Matt Stone's a dangerous man.'

'I can take care of Stone.'

Braddock didn't answer for a moment. He had formulated a plan during his ride up the mountain and his mind was still going over necessary details. He took a sip of whiskey and wiped his mouth with the back of his hand. 'We've got another problem. We can't trust Kimball any longer. He's actin' like a rabbit in the middle of a pack of wolves. It wouldn't take much to get him to talk. It's time we got get rid of him.'

'How do you want me to handle it?'

'I've been thinking on that,' Braddock replied. 'Including Stone, we've got two problems so we might as well take care of both of them at the same time.' He took another drink as he considered the details of his plan. 'We're short right now so we'll wait a week or two. Five men will be back from the drive by then, and I want you to hire another three or four guns.' Braddock looked straight at Caldwell. 'My plan will take perfect timing so you'd better not bungle it. If you do it right, both of our problems will be out of the way – permanently.'

Matt enjoyed a day of rest while recovering from his ordeal. He could have taken more time but he was concerned about the outlaws and eager to begin his new job. The following morning, he reported to Tom Kimball to learn of his particular duties on the ranch, but he was told to report directly to Colby instead. He reached the house and the major greeted him at the door.

'Join me for breakfast, Matt. I want to talk to you.'

Matt accepted the invitation and the two walked into the dining room. He entered the room and saw that they would be alone for breakfast. This made him believe Colby had a serious discussion in mind. The two men ate and talked about a variety of things, but Matt sensed that Colby was waiting for the right time to speak about something in particular.

Colby finished his meal, shoved his plate away, and placed his coffee cup where the plate had been. He swirled his spoon around the cup several times, then looked across the table. 'Matt, those Mosquito Creek outlaws have been causing a lot of trouble and it's only going to get worse. I know I hired you on as a cowhand but I want to give you a different job for now.'

'I'm not sure I understand.'

'I didn't expect you to. What I've got in mind is a bit unusual, but I think it's necessary.' Colby got up, walked to the window and clasped his hands behind his back. 'I'm very concerned about my family. They already took Katie once and there's no telling what they might do next.'

'I'm worried about that myself.'

Colby turned and looked directly at Matt. 'I admire the way you handle yourself in tough situations. I've got a special job and I think you're the right man.'

'What'd you have in mind?'

'I want to put you in charge of security, but I don't mean it in the normal sense of the word. I'm talking about my ranch *and* my family.'

Matt was somewhat surprised by the major's statement. He had only known the man a few days, and he was now being asked to take on a position of high trust. He considered the situation a moment before answering. 'What about your foreman or some of the others?'

'Kimball? Well, he's a good enough foreman, but he doesn't seem to be up to the heavier matters. Fact is, he always seems to be in the wrong place when we have trouble. I'm beginning to think he's afraid to mix it up with those outlaws.' Colby paused, then added. 'I get the feeling you don't wish to have a conflict with Kimball concerning ranch duties. I'd expect that from you. After all, you arrived only a short time ago.'

Matt nodded. 'Something like that.'

'Don't worry, I'll talk to Tom. And I can guarantee there won't be any problems.'

Matt put down his cup and thought about the offer. He knew Colby's wife would be back in a few weeks, and he was already concerned for the safety of Laura and Katie. The more he thought about it the more sense it made. He made a quick decision. 'I'll do it on two conditions.'

'Name them.'

'Me and Spider work as partners. I'd want him on the same job.'

'Done. What else?'

'I'll certainly check with you before doing anything out of the ordinary, but I want everyone to know I'm in charge of security. What I say goes.'

'That's fine with me. Just as long as you keep me informed.'

Matt extended his hand. 'I wouldn't have it any other way.'

Colby seemed relieved as he shook hands with Matt. 'It's taken me a long time to build up this ranch and I'm not about to let outlaws ruin all that work. But you must understand one thing – my family comes first. I'll do whatever it takes to protect them.'

'As I see it, Major, the first thing we've got to do is weed out your spy.'

Colby appeared bewildered. 'You think one of my men is on their payroll?'

'No doubt about it. You told me they always strike

where you and other ranchers have the fewest men. They also knew we took the Loop and ambushed us with a large force. It adds up to one thing. They've got somebody on the inside.'

Colby obviously had trouble accepting the idea that one of his own men would turn on him, but as Matt continued laying out the facts there was only one conclusion any man could reach. Colby finally shook his head. 'You're right, Matt. I don't know why I didn't see it myself. I guess I just didn't want to.'

'We'll find out who it is, but to end this thing for good we've got to find out who's behind that gang and where their hideout is.'

'The hideout's on Bear Mountain. I'm sure of it. You'll hear the townsfolk call it Death Mountain, but I refuse to use that name. It's gotten so bad the sheriff won't send men up there anymore. Too many of them don't come back and they've never been able to find a thing. People are downright scared of the place.'

'Major,' Matt replied, 'I can promise you we'll find the hideout. It may take a while but we'll find it.' Matt paused as he thought about the outlaws, and then said. 'Do you have any idea who's behind this gang?'

'I know Jace Caldwell and that bunch he hangs out with him at the Dog Head Saloon are involved, but we can't prove it.'

'Jace is a tough *hombre*,' Matt said, 'but he's not smart enough to have organized this.'

Colby fell silent for a moment. 'It's someone else . . . but I have no idea who.'

The following week, Matt put considerable effort into preparing the Box C for any eventuality. He went about his task in a detailed and organized manner. One of his first concerns was the amount and condition of all weapons on the ranch. After his inspection, he ordered several new rifles and additional ammunition. Standing orders were put out for all firearms to be cleaned and maintained in proper condition – and they were to be kept close at hand.

One of Matt's tasks was to survey the cattle herds. He felt it was important to distribute the men according to the cattle population in each region. He implemented a procedure to try to maintain proper coverage at all times, but the ranch was short-handed. Matt and Spider also began to make frequent rides over the entire ranch, and no one but Colby knew where they might turn up at any given time. They made a few trips into the lower sections of the mountains, but did not venture too far as they wanted to stay reasonably close to those they were to protect at the ranch.

They had just returned from a routine scouting trip when they saw a rider closing on the ranch at a fast pace. It was Gus Knox. Knox yelled as he jumped from his horse. 'Where's the major?'

'Inside,' someone answered. 'I'll get him.'

Colby heard his name and stepped off the porch. 'What's wrong, Gus?'

'They hit us just before sunrise. They got a bunch of cattle.'

'Anyone hurt?'

'Barney's shot up bad. There were only three of us out there. Bill's takin' him into town.'

Anger flashed on Colby's face.

'We goin' after them, Boss?'

Colby rubbed his chin. 'No, by the time we get back out there they'll be up in those mountains. It's a death trap up there. We'll figure something out tomorrow.'

Matt discussed the new attack with Colby, then he remained on the porch a few minutes after the others had gone back into the house. He was trying to think of a way to counter the mounting attacks on the Box C. As he stood against the rail, a boy who looked about fifteen came across the yard and spoke to him. 'Are you Matt Stone?'

'I'm Stone.'

'A man in town paid me to deliver this message to you.'

The boy handled him a sealed envelope and walked away. Matt opened the envelope and read the message.

I know where the Mosquito Creek outlaw's hideout is. Meet me at the edge of the trees behind the Dog Head Saloon at sunset tomorrow. Come alone or I won't show.

CHAPTER 14

Fats Braddock sat at a corner table in the Dog Head Saloon and lit a cigarette. He blew a dense cloud of smoke across the table, then leaned back to consider recent events. Reports of the raid on Colby's Box C were good. He had sent for Jace Caldwell and sipped whiskey while he waited. His thoughts turned to the future as they often did in recent days. His original plan was to slowly take over the town, and then squeeze profits from every possible source, but the robberies and cattle raids he had ordered across the region in recent months had been more lucrative than even he had expected. Braddock had always had another plan in the back of his mind and each day the alternate plan gained appeal. If he could gather enough money, he had often thought of moving to a large eastern city where he could enjoy the life of a rich man in elegant surroundings. This goal seemed more desirable each day.

His rule over the outlaws was that of a tyrant, and no one questioned him for fear of death. Most of the men had either heard of or seen him shoot a man for the slightest of reasons. And Jace Caldwell was always there to back him up. Braddock examined his situation. All of the money came to him and no one else had any idea of how much had been accumulated. He portioned out money and other favours in just the right amounts to keep his men happy, but all the while his personal accounts grew steadily.

Braddock lifted his glass and finished the contents. When he placed the glass back on the table he had reached a decision. Within a few months, he would have sufficient funds to move to the East and live in style. He would say he was travelling to Denver on business and simply keep going. Caldwell and the others would never venture to the East in search of him. In fact, he was sure they wouldn't have the slightest idea where he was. A smile crossed Braddock's face – he would be set for life.

But there were certain obstacles in his way. Braddock knew Matt Stone was dangerous, and Kimball was a weak link. Braddock's plan to eliminate both of them had already begun. Caldwell had paid a boy to deliver the note to Stone, and Braddock thought he would take the bait.

Jace Caldwell entered the saloon, scanned the room, and then made his way toward the table.

'Everything set?' Braddock asked.

'Just like you said.'

'Any trouble with Kimball?'

'Naw. I told him to meet you out back just before sunset.' Caldwell picked up a glass and poured a drink. 'He's sure got a scared look in his eyes lately.'

Braddock didn't answer for a few seconds. He sucked on his cigarette and exhaled the smoke through his nostrils. 'That's why we've got to get rid of him. He'll break the first time somebody puts him under pressure. We can't take a chance of that happening.'

'Yeah, he'd point a finger at us real quick.'

'Not after today,' Braddock answered. 'If we do this right, we'll be rid of both of 'em and no one will be suspicious of us. It's only a couple of hours till sunset. Go out back and make sure everything is set.'

*

Matt had not told anyone about the note. He was aware that whoever had sent him the note could be setting up a trap, but he also felt there was a good chance the note might be legitimate. The fact that the unknown person wanted to meet him in town made the message seem more authentic. If someone wanted to set up an ambush it seemed more likely they would pick a lonely spot away from town. He decided to take Spider to Benbow but not tell him of the note. He knew Spider would demand to be involved. If this was a legitimate informer, Matt did not want to take any chance of missing the opportunity.

He walked around the corner of the barn and saw Laura waving to someone. Matt glanced down the road and saw Tom Kimball riding in the direction of town. He looked for Spider and found him in the barn. 'Saddle up. We're going into Benbow for a while.'

'How soon?'

'Thirty minutes.'

They arrived in Benbow about an hour before sunset. Matt told Spider he would meet him in an hour for a drink. Then he tied his horse on the opposite side of the street, retrieved a second revolver from his saddlebags and shoved it under his belt. He looked up and down the street but saw nothing unusual. He would not be satisfied with a single observation and decided to use the remaining time before sunset to walk the length of the street and look for anything suspicious. He noticed there were more horses in town than usual, but nothing else appeared out of the ordinary.

He completed his inspection and stopped about a hundred yards from the Dog Head Saloon. He was on the opposite side of the street and could easily see any activity in the immediate area. He watched the street until the sun approached the mountains. There was an alley next to the Dog Head, and Matt knew he would be expected to walk through it to get to the back but this seemed too dangerous. He decided to use a small alley farther up the street and then go along the back of the buildings until he came opposite the designated meeting place behind the saloon.

Just before the appointed time, Matt made his way across the street and into the alley, using extreme caution as he approached the rear of the buildings. He saw nothing unusual and took a quick glance around the corner of the building. There was no one in sight. He waited a few minutes but saw no movement. As he was about to step out, a door opened on one of the buildings next to him. He moved back and watched as a shopkeeper stacked a small crate against a wall behind his place of business. Nothing unusual in that – everything seemed normal.

Matt squinted and scanned the trees. He couldn't see anyone in that direction, but he did not expect to. Whoever sent the note would not show himself until he knew Matt had followed instructions and come alone. At the appointed time, he checked his weapons and began moving across the narrow strip between the row of buildings and the trees. He was still about seventy yards from the rear of the saloon when he came to the first row of trees. He moved slowly along the edge of the wooded slope until he was thirty yards away from his destination. He stopped and looked around, but there was still no sign of anyone at the meeting site. More than half of the sun was now below the mountain tops. Matt grew uneasy and thought of turning back – it just didn't feel right.

Suddenly, he caught a glimpse of someone standing just inside the trees. It appeared to be one person, but he knew there could be any number of men hidden on the tree-covered slope. He checked the surroundings again, then worked along the edge of the trees and approached the spot where he had seen movement. Someone stepped behind a tree. Matt thought he recognized Tom Kimball.

'Tom, is that you?'

No answer. Matt drew his pistol and stepped next to one of the trees. He tried again. 'Kimball?'

After a few seconds, Tom Kimball stepped out from behind a tree and walked toward Matt. 'What are you doing here?' Kimball asked.

'I got a message to meet someone here who had information on the outlaws.'

When Kimball heard those words he shouted, 'It's a set-up!'

There was a rustling sound from the trees on the slope. Just as Kimball looked in the direction of the noise the boom of a gun broke the stillness of the early evening air. A second shot quickly followed. The first bullet hit Kimball causing his body to twist slightly. The second spun him completely around and he fell heavily to the ground.

Two more shots were fired and bullets dug into the dirt next to Matt. He saw a shadow move up the slope from one of the trees and he fired at the movement. Another bullet hit a tree next to him and Matt responded with two more shots, but he couldn't see his targets. There were obviously several men in the trees, so he turned to run toward the buildings. Just as he started, he saw three men on his right step from behind an out-building, their rifles levelled on him. He turned to his left only to see three more step from the alley he had used earlier.

'Dammit, I should have known.'

The odds were bad, but Matt decided to make a run for

the alley next to the saloon. It was directly in front of him and about forty yards away. After he had covered about fifteen yards, he was surprised that no one had fired on him. He was a little over halfway to the buildings when he saw four men hurry around the corner and enter the alley from the street. Matt stopped in his tracks – he was now completely surrounded. He pulled the second gun from his belt and prepared for the worst, expecting a bullet to smash into him any second.

The sun was going down but there was still good light. He looked hard at the men and felt relief when he recognized Sheriff Potter.

The sheriff yelled out, 'Hold your fire everybody! Hold your fire!' The sheriff moved to within a few steps away from Matt and asked, 'What's all the shooting about?'

Before Matt could answer, one of the men off to the side yelled, 'Watch him, Sheriff! We just saw him plug Tom Kimball. He's lying right over there.'

'What?' the sheriff yelled. He seemed stunned by the man's declaration. Potter stepped aside to look in the direction the man had pointed. When he saw the crumpled body, he started toward the downed man. 'Take his guns and hold him here.'

Matt was surrounded by ten men and had no choice but to surrender his weapons. The men that stood around him were not those that made up the citizenry of the town; instead, they were mostly rough men who hung out at the Dog Head Saloon. Matt became furious with himself for falling into such an obvious trap.

While he waited for the sheriff to return he saw several other men come out the back of the saloon. Jace Caldwell was among them. The big gunman laughed loudly as he pointed at Matt.

Just as the sheriff stood up and began to walk back to the group, Spider McCaw came through the alley on the run. When he saw the group holding guns on Matt, he stopped short. He then saw Caldwell drinking from a whiskey bottle and laughing.

Spider yelled at the assembled group. 'What's going on here?'

Caldwell was the first to answer. 'Your partner just killed Tom Kimball and he's gonna hang for it.' Caldwell again broke into laughter and hurled the empty bottle toward the trees.

Spider's right hand dropped and he spun toward Caldwell.

Sheriff Potter had been watching and yelled, 'Spider! Hold on.' The sheriff ran toward him with his arms extended and his palms down. 'Keep that pistol in your holster. We don't know what happened here but I mean to find out. You'll only make it worse by pulling your gun.' The sheriff continued motioning with his hands. 'Don't touch that gun.'

Matt yelled at Spider. 'There are too many of them. Do as he says.'

Though reluctant, Spider moved his hand from his holster and turned away from Caldwell.

Matt called to him. 'Get word to Colby.'

Caldwell yelled to the two men. 'Nobody's gonna be able to help you now, Stone. You're gonna hang.'

Spider's anger boiled as he watched the sheriff guide Matt toward the jail. He was considering ways to help his friend, but he needed details about what happened. He glanced around the crowd and saw a shopkeeper he and Matt had befriended. Spider remembered seeing the man behind the saloon when he first came through the alley.

He waved at the shopkeeper and walked toward him. 'Ben, what happened back there?'

'Well, Spider, all I know is what I heard.'

'Did you hear Matt's side of it?'

'Not much, but I did hear him say Kimball was killed by gunmen from the trees. Matt said they fired on him and he shot back.'

Spider glanced toward the tree-covered slope. The area was not too steep and riders could easily follow the terrain into the foothills. He turned back to Ben. 'Can I borrow a lantern?'

'Sure, but it'd be suicide to go after them in those trees . . . especially with a lamp.'

'It's the only chance Matt's got. I've got to try and catch one of them.'

A few minutes later, Spider was searching the trees behind the Dog Head Saloon. He found several boot imprints in the dirt, but no shell casings or horse tracks could be found. He followed the boot markings up the hill and saw where the killers had attempted to cover their tracks. It was obvious the shooting had been carefully planned. The gunmen had not only picked up their spent cartridges, they had also kept their horses at a distance.

Spider followed what was left of the tracks. He knew the lantern made him an easy target, but he anticipated that the gunmen had orders to flee the area quickly. He moved through the trees with the lantern in one hand and the horse's reins in the other. After fifteen minutes, he found where the horses had been tied. There was no longer any attempt to hide the tracks, and it appeared that five or six men had been involved. Spider remounted and followed the markings, leaning to one side, holding the lantern low as he went. The trees began to thin and the terrain became rougher. Feeling uneasy, Spider set the lantern on a large rock and circled the area. He noticed a narrow gap bordered by a craggy wall on one side and large boulders on the other. The passage was directly in line with the direction the tracks had taken, but he knew they could have easily changed directions.

Spider went back for the lantern and continued tracking. He was twenty yards from two large boulders when shots rang out. The first bullet nicked the back of his saddle, the second whistled past his ear. He bolted his horse into the trees and dismounted. He crouched behind a tree and aimed his rifle toward the top of the boulders in time to see a flash from another shot. He quickly placed two shots toward the flash, then rolled over to another tree. Several bullets dug into the ground next to the tree he had just left. Spider again aimed at the flashes and rapidly sent three shots toward the top of the boulders, one on the right side of the flash and two on the left. On his last shot, he heard a man cry out in pain. The shooting stopped.

Spider thought this odd because he had been following the tracks of at least five men, and that many gunmen would have sent a heavy barrage of shots at him. They must have left one or two behind to protect the trail, but he could not be sure. He waited several minutes, but no more shots were fired. He finally moved to his left and crossed into rocks and heavy brush. He continued to the left, circling toward the side of the boulders.

He heard something and stopped short. Tilting his head, he made out the muffled sound of at least one horse moving away from him. Spider waited a moment, then continued moving in a manner that put him on the opposite side of the boulders. It was difficult to see, but as he inched forward he could make out the rough outline of a single man crumpled on top of one of the large rocks. Spider waited, but noticed no movement or sounds from the boulders or the surrounding area. When he felt safe he moved into the rocks with his rifle at the ready. Other than the man he had seen, there was no one there. He climbed the rock and, having determined that the man was dead, he backtracked and got his lantern.

Several minutes later, he inspected the boulders with a dim light. From the tracks and the number of spent cartridges he determined that only two gunmen had been waiting for him. He followed their footprints and located a horse tied to a tree. A single question held Spider's thoughts. Were these two with the killers who gunned down Tom Kimball, or were they a separate group whose only objective was to cover the escape route of the others? After following the trail the two men had used to reach the boulders, Spider soon had his answer. These men had come in from a different direction. Their tracks did not meet up with the larger group.

Discouraged, Spider went back to the gap where he had last seen the original tracks. He had lost valuable time and knew his chances of catching one of the murderous gunmen were remote. Still, he meant to follow them, hoping to get lucky. The tracks continued through the foothills for about three miles, then made a wide sweep to the left and angled back toward the valley floor. Spider followed the trail until he came out of the trees about two miles north of town. When their strategy became obvious, he stopped and muttered to himself. 'Dammit. . . . They're going right back to town.'

He soon reached the main road and saw that the markings he followed disappeared among dozens of tracks. He spurred his horse and galloped toward town. The killers had made a wide circle, and Spider suspected they had gone right back to the Dog Head Saloon. He entered town cautiously, scanning the street as he rode. He stopped across the street from the saloon and glanced around. The street was now full of horses. Loud noises carried out of the Dog Head and could be heard for some distance. Spider's search was over and he knew there was nothing he could do.

He decided to stay in town and spend the next morning talking to everyone on the street. Perhaps a shopkeeper saw what happened. The chances were not good but he had to try. If this failed he would consider other methods to free his friend.

CHAPTER 15

The news that Tom Kimball was dead, and Matt had been arrested for the murder jolted the Colby family. Shock and disbelief gripped everyone. The news had reached the ranch at night, causing Colby and Laura to stay up late. Katie would not be told until the next morning. Major Colby had not known Matt Stone long, but he believed in the man and considered him a friend. But he also knew Matt had been caught with a dead body and a smoking gun. Although the many witnesses who came forth were of dubious character, they were witnesses nonetheless. Matt was in a tight spot.

Laura was devastated by the news. Of the two men that she had an interest in, one was dead and the other was in jail charged with murder. Her thoughts ranged from confusion to sorrow. She found it hard to believe that Matt would have shot Tom in cold blood. Her instincts about Matt's character were strong, but how could she be sure? It was late when Laura went across the main room and sat next to her father.

They talked some until her father said, 'Why don't you try to get some sleep?'

'I'll just lay up there wide awake. I'd rather be down here with you.'

They were quiet for a time until Colby broke the

111

silence. 'Laura, if Tom's time had to come, maybe it's best that it happened before you were married. It would have been harder on you later.'

Laura did not answer for a moment, then she looked at him and said, 'I haven't told you this but I was beginning to have doubts. Tom had been changing . . . he was pulling away. It's hard to explain but he just wasn't the same.' She paused. 'He wanted to announce our engagement but I just couldn't do it.'

Major Colby told Katie about the shooting early the next morning. Of all the members of the Colby family, Katie knew Matt was innocent. There was no other answer. She simply knew he was not guilty. Katie thought hard about Matt's predicament before she decided to act. Someone had to help him and she thought it should be her. Her father was going to town later that day, and she hoped to convince him to let her go along. With her plan decided on, Katie went into the kitchen and began to bake a cake. She watched for her father and Laura while she scurried about the kitchen, waiting for both of them to be outside at the same time. When her cake was in the oven, Katie got her chance.

She ran to her father's office and went to the cabinet where he stored extra guns. She swung the door open and searched for the smallest pistol she could find. She found a short-barrelled Colt that still seemed huge to her, then she grabbed a handful of cartridges and ran up the stairs toward her room. Katie searched through her dresser and took out several long ribbons. She tied them together and then took off her dress. She wrapped the long ribbon around her waist and slipped the end through the trigger guard on the pistol, then repeated the process to make sure the ribbon would not break. After the gun was tightly strapped to her waist, she put on a more loosely fitting dress. She placed a pinafore over the dress.

At first, her father would not let Katie accompany him to Benbow. But Katie expected that, and after explaining she had baked a small cake for Matt, her father relented. With an escort of two ranch hands, they left in a buckboard well before noon.

Matt got less than three hours of sleep during the night. Spider came by early and was now out talking to everyone in town, trying to find other witnesses to the shooting. It was late morning and Matt had still not seen the sheriff. He was pacing about his cell when Potter finally came through the door from his office. Matt had not talked with the sheriff since he was locked up the previous evening and was anxious for news, hoping someone might have come forward on his behalf.

The sheriff spoke first. 'Mornin', Matt. I don't suppose you got much sleep last night.'

Matt ignored the greeting and went right to the important matters at hand. 'I didn't kill him, Sheriff. You must know that.'

'I'd like to believe you but I've got to go on facts. And the facts stack up against you.'

'Have you checked for other witnesses? Maybe a shopkeeper saw something.'

'That's the first thing I did this morning, but you're not going to like what I found.' The sheriff hesitated before letting out a heavy sigh. 'None of them saw the shooting, but a few rushed to look after they heard the shots. All they could say was that you were standing near the body and there was heavy gunsmoke all around.'

'Hell, Sheriff, someone shot him from the trees. They shot at me too so I fired back.'

'But you can't prove that.'

'What about those witnesses behind the saloon. They're

113

nothing but a bunch of outlaws. You know it and I know it.'

'You're right, but until they're proven guilty of something their word will hold up in court.'

Matt's predicament suddenly became more urgent. Whoever set him up had covered every detail. Without a witness on his behalf he would have little chance in court.

The sheriff moved closer to his cell and spoke in a sincere tone. 'I'll keep trying. You've got my word on it.' Potter turned and started toward the door but stopped as if he had an afterthought, then he walked back to Matt's cell. 'One more thing: Tom was still alive when I got to him.'

Matt's head shot up and he quickly moved to the cell door. 'Did he say anything?'

'He only lasted a few seconds.'

'Did he talk?'

'Yeah, he said a few things, but I couldn't understand most of it. All I could make out was something about Rattlesnake Canyon, but that doesn't make any sense. The only time you can get into that snake-infested canyon is in the winter. Besides, it's a box canyon. There's only one way in or out.'

'Did he say anything else?'

'I think he tried to say someone's name but I couldn't make it out.'

'Nothing else?'

'Like I said, I couldn't make out the rest. It was just a weak mumble.'

When the sheriff left, Matt went over everything he had just learned, his mind carefully analysing every detail. He was looking for a way out – some clue that would enable him to get free. But his thoughts kept returning to Rattlesnake Canyon. That was near where he and Spider had lost the tracks of Jarrod Kern's killers. What was

Kimball trying to tell the sheriff? It had to have something to do with the outlaws or their hideout. There would be no other reason for a dying man to mention such a place. Matt grabbed hold of the cell bars and lowered his head in despair. Even if their hideout was near Rattlesnake Canyon there was nothing he could do about it. He could tell Spider, but Matt desperately needed to get out of jail.

He was sitting on his bunk when he heard voices from the sheriff's office. He recognized Major Colby's voice and hoped his visitor brought good news. A moment later, the door opened and Katie was the first to enter. She carried a plate covered by a red cloth. Matt noticed that her usual broad smile was missing. She was followed by her father and the sheriff.

Once inside the room, Katie forced a smile and tried to show her usual cheerfulness. 'Mr Stone. I . . . I brought you a cake. I hope you like it.'

'Why, Katie, that was awful nice of you.'

'She got up this morning and baked it herself,' Colby said. He then looked Matt in the eye. 'How are you holding up?'

'Looks like they've set me up pretty good, Major. I've been in better spots.'

While the two men talked about the events of the previous evening, Katie set the cake down and nervously waited for them to finish.

When the discussion was over, Colby turned to Katie. 'Just leave that cake for Matt. It's time to go.'

Katie pleaded with her father. 'Daddy, I want to stay and eat a piece of cake with Mr Stone. Is that all right, Sheriff?'

'Well . . . I guess if it's all right with your father, it's OK with me. But just for a little while.'

Katie looked at her father with the most pleading look she could muster. 'Please, Daddy.'

'All right, I'll be back in thirty minutes.'

Sheriff Potter spoke as he turned toward the door, 'I can't let you keep a knife in here, Katie, but I'll bring one in and cut a few pieces of that cake for you.'

'Thank you, Sheriff.'

The sheriff came back to cut the cake, then he returned to his office.

As soon as the door was closed, Katie went into action.

Matt was astounded as he watched Katie hurriedly take off her pinafore and then lift up her dress. 'Katie, what are you doing?' Just as the last word rolled off his lips he saw the gun. Matt was stunned. This nine-year-old girl had packed a Colt revolver into the jail right under the sheriff's nose. As Matt stared in disbelief, Katie slipped off one shoe and removed a small pocket knife. She then sliced the ribbon and the gun fell to the floor with a loud thud.

Matt glanced toward the door while Katie kicked the gun under the bars and into his cell. He grabbed the gun and placed it under his mattress; then he turned to Katie. 'Cartridges?'

Katie reached into her pocket and produced a handful of shells and handed them through the bars.

Matt shook his head as he looked at the remarkable girl with long curly hair and freckled nose. 'Katie, you're some special young lady.' He paused a few seconds. 'You could get into a lot of trouble for this.'

'I know, but I also know you're innocent. And besides, you saved my life.'

'All right, but don't tell anyone but Spider. Not anyone, not even your dad for now. You can tell him tomorrow. He's going to be mad but I'll fix it for you later. Can you do that?'

'Yes.' Her belief in Matt came through in her voice.

'All right. Now listen carefully. Spider's here in town. You've got to find him and tell him to bring two horses to the back of the jail just before midnight. Tell him that's when the deputy came in from rounds last night. If he doesn't show at the same time tonight, tell Spider to wait till he does.'

'I'll tell him.' Katie suddenly looked down at her dress as though she had forgotten something. She then reached into her pocket and withdrew an object, which she handed to Matt. 'I found this arrowhead in the valley and it's always brought me good luck. I want you to have it.'

'You're a blessing, Katie.'

The last two days had been hot and today was worse. Matt sweated through the long afternoon and evening hours in his stuffy cell. Time seemed to drag. But when his patience wore thin, he would remove Katie's good-luck piece from his pocket and roll it around in his hand. He still marvelled at her fortitude. When the sun finally went down, Matt began his long wait until the deputy would return from his evening rounds. Midnight finally came, but there was no sign of the lawman. The minutes ticked by and Matt grew increasing impatient. At twelve-thirty, there was still no sign of the deputy. Matt paced the floor until nearly one o'clock when he heard a commotion on the street. He checked his gun and replaced it under his belt near the middle of his back.

The noises grew louder and now came from inside the sheriff's office. A few seconds later, the door to the cells opened and the lawman came in manoeuvring a drunken cowboy toward the cells. The man was loud, belligerent, and staggering so badly he could barely walk. The deputy shoved the drunk into the cell next to Matt. 'He's noisy now, but he'll most likely go right to sleep.'

Matt did not reply, but when the deputy turned toward the door he pulled his gun and spoke firmly. 'Don't turn around.' He then cocked his revolver to let the deputy know he was armed. The noise froze the man in his tracks.

Matt spoke quickly. 'If you do as I say you won't get hurt. Now back up real slow.' When the lawman backed up against the bars, Matt grabbed his gun. He shoved the weapon into his belt and then reached for the man's keys. After opening the door, Matt exchanged places with the deputy and locked the cell door. He opened the office door and looked back. 'If you start making noise, I'll come back to shut you up. Understand?'

The deputy nodded grimly.

Matt went outside and found the street to be nearly deserted. He ran to the alley and made his way between the buildings. He reached the rear of the structures and paused a few seconds to let his eyes adjust to the dark. After a moment, he ran directly behind the jail. He went about twenty yards and sent out a low whistle.

'Over here.' It was Spider's voice.

Matt ran toward the sound, located his horse, and sprang into the saddle. They had no trouble escaping from town, but they rode hard for thirty minutes just to be safe. Spider had been in the lead and was headed toward the Box C when Matt yelled out. 'Hold up. We're not going to the ranch.' They pulled to a stop.

'Where are we going?'

'Death Mountain.'

CHAPTER 16

After Katie and her father had left for town, Laura Colby began to wish she had gone along. As the day progressed, she had become more concerned for Matt's welfare and she now felt sure of one thing – Matt was not the type of person who would murder anyone. No matter what the evidence indicated, she believed in him. She also felt guilty about her feelings toward Tom Kimball because she believed her sorrow for him should have been deeper even though she knew she would never have agreed to the marriage.

An hour before sunset, Laura paced back and forth on the porch, looking in the distance, expecting her father's return at any moment. After again searching the road she decided to ride out a short distance and meet Katie and her father. There was a small, tree-covered knoll not far from the house that offered a good view of the main road to Benbow. Laura went across the yard and spoke to Fuzzy Thurman. 'I'm going to ride out to the knoll and wait for Dad.'

Fuzzy stopped working and looked up. 'I can't let you go out there alone. Somebody's got to go with you or I'll catch it.' He called back as he entered the barn. 'I'll saddle the horses.'

The sun was nearing the top of the mountains when they reached their destination overlooking the intersection of the road to town and a trail that turned south and entered the mountains. The site was near the foothills and offered a good view of the valley.

Laura pointed toward dust in the distance. 'There they are.'

Fuzzy's experienced eyes swept over the valley and settled on the dust. 'That ain't them, Laura. Too many riders. I'm moving our horses back a bit. Stay out of sight.' He returned and scanned the area. 'We've got a bad set-up here. Look at the mountain trail.'

Laura glanced up the trail and saw two riders coming out of the foothills not more than two-hundred feet away.

Fuzzy cocked his rifle. 'They aren't friendlies. You stay down and don't make a sound. If they spot us, you get to your horse and make for the ranch. Don't look back. Just go flat out.'

Laura watched anxiously as the pair stopped at the intersection just below the knoll. A few minutes later, the four riders from the valley road pulled to a stop.

Fuzzy whispered. 'It's Fats Braddock and Jace Caldwell.'

Braddock was the first to speak. 'Where're you two headed?'

'We been in that hole for a week and we thought we'd go into Benbow.'

Braddock answered swiftly. 'Not tonight. We've got work to do.'

'What's up?'

'We just got rid of two problems and we're going to make the most of it. Some of our boys shot Kimball and we made it look like Matt Stone did it. Kimball's been a help to us but he was getting shaky. Now we don't have to worry about either one of them.'

Laughter made its way up the hill to Laura's ears. She

was stunned by the news but she was also scared. The mysterious leader of the Mosquito Creek outlaws was right below her. She knew these men were ruthless and would show no mercy to anyone who overheard them.

Braddock gave orders. 'I want everybody back at the hideout. We're going to step up our raids. We're going to hit that bank in Everett and the one in Benbow. There'll be a nice pay-off in it for you boys.'

Just as Braddock finished, a twig snapped behind Laura. A voice sounded from their rear. 'Don't move!'

Fuzzy shoved Laura to the ground and then spun around and fired a shot. At the same instant, a bullet zinged by his head. His second shot caught the gunman in the head just as he looked out from behind a tree. The man crumpled to the ground.

Fuzzy yelled at Laura. 'Run! Get out of here!'

Laura ran toward her horse and heard a barrage of gunfire. She mounted, looked back, and yelled. 'Fuzzy, don't stay! Fuzzy!'

He continued firing at the men without looking at her. 'Get outta here – now!'

Laura guided her horse down the knoll and was soon racing across the flats. She had been told not to look back, but she had to. She turned just in time to see Fuzzy ride down the knoll. Heavy rifle fire erupted as she watched. Fuzzy slumped in his saddle and his horse veered off to one side. More shots were fired and his horse was struck. The animal fell heavily throwing the rider to the ground. Fuzzy did not get up.

She raced toward the ranch, her fear changing to concern for Fuzzy. The knoll was just over a mile from the ranch complex and it appeared she had enough head-start to make it safely, but she was deeply distressed about Fuzzy. She was also concerned about the ranch. She pulled the carbine out of the boot and fired two warning shots. She neared the barn and saw Punch Mitchell run out the back of the building with his revolver drawn.

She pulled to a stop, sending dust flying.

Punch shouted. 'What's wrong?'

Before she could answer, another man came around the side of the barn carrying a Winchester.

'They shot Fuzzy!' she yelled.

'What? Who?'

Laura dismounted and looked toward the knoll. As soon as she was satisfied the gunmen were not bearing down on the ranch she related the details of what had happened. She told of overhearing Fats Braddock and Jace Caldwell. When she finished, she looked in the direction of the knoll. 'We've got to help Fuzzy.'

Mitchell stepped closer and softened his tone. 'Laura, if Caldwell's in that bunch.' He stopped for a second, obviously trying to pick the right words. 'What I'm trying to say is that Fuzzy won't be coming back.'

Laura intuitively knew he was dead, but the words made the truth strike even harder. She was silent for a moment, then lifted her head. 'What about Dad? Can we send some men out?'

'We've only got three here now and I've got orders to keep them here. Besides, he's got two good men with him. They'll be all right.'

Darkness was descending over the valley when Laura walked to the house. She started through the front door but changed her mind and decided to wait on the porch. She stared out at the darkening valley and struggled with her thoughts. It was nearly an hour before the buckboard pulled into the ranch yard. Laura and Punch Mitchell were standing in the middle of the yard when the wagon stopped. Major Colby was visibly upset with the news. He paced back and forth beside the buckboard for several minutes without speaking. He then knelt in front of his youngest daughter. 'Katie, I want you to go inside, eat supper, and then go on up to bed.'

She nodded.

'I don't want you going out of the ranch yard for the next few days. This is very important. Do you promise?'

Katie seemed to understand how serious things were becoming. 'I promise.'

When Katie had left, Colby turned to the small group gathered in the yard. 'Well, boys, looks like a war is brewing. Our people are the most important things right now. Punch, send out the word. To hell with the cattle. Call everybody in.'

'What about Matt?' Laura said. 'Shouldn't we send someone to tell the sheriff what I heard?'

'It won't do any good tonight because they have all of those witnesses against Matt. The sheriff can't let him out. As far as the bank is concerned, we just don't know what the outlaws will do. If they think you heard them they'll hold off, but we'll send someone in early just in case.' Colby put his arm around Laura and started toward the house. He walked a few steps, then stopped and turned. 'Punch, I want extra guards out every night from now on.'

Laura and her father sat for a long time over supper, but neither ate much. They talked a little about Fuzzy Thurman, but they were mostly silent, each dealing with the loss as best they could. After supper, Laura hoped reading would give her mind a respite from the violent events of the last few days, but she was unable to concentrate – her thoughts kept going back to the tragedy on the knoll.

It was late when she finally said good night to her father. He looked tired and troubled as he sat at his large desk. She bent over and kissed him on the cheek, then went upstairs. As tired as she was, Laura could not sleep. She again thought about the day's events, but she also thought about Matt. Surely there was a way to get him out of jail – there had to be. Laura was unaware of Katie's courageous actions earlier in the day.

CHAPTER 17

After the brief skirmish at the knoll, Braddock's first thought was to send his men after Colby's daughter but he knew it was too late. Unsure of how many men were on the Box C, Braddock decided the risk was too high for an attack. Besides, he thought, the man with her was dead and he did not think she had heard anything. Braddock had more important things to accomplish. He had recently decided to move his personal timetable forward. He meant to send his men on several raids, and then carry out his plan to go to Denver on business. Two men would accompany him as usual, but he intended to disappear while they slept. He would then go east and live in comfort. No one would ever find him. He rode along the mountain trail and continued to review his plans. Braddock had earlier given orders for most of his men to gather at the hideout and await instructions. He planned to send them out in two or three days with orders to strike several targets. As usual, he would wait in his cabin. Each raid would bring him closer to his goal, closer to a life of luxury.

It was after midnight when he and his men reached the hideout. When they were sure no one was in the area, the heavy plank was lowered from the tunnel entrance, and the outlaws entered the shaft in single file. After a difficult dismount, Braddock yelled at Caldwell. 'Jace, I need to talk to you.' He walked into the room, rolled a cigarette, and sat behind the table.

Caldwell entered and poured a whiskey. 'What's on your mind?'

'You know those bank jobs I've been talking about? It's time. We'll split our men into two groups. I want you to send one bunch to Everett as soon as the rest of our men arrive. They should be ready to go in two or three days. I want you to take the others and hit the bank in Benbow the same day. Don't do that job yourself, and make sure the men you pick are unknown in town.' He tapped his fingers on the table. 'One more thing. Have someone kill the sheriff.'

'I'll handle the sheriff myself,' the big gunman replied. A smile came to his lips. 'Then I'll go in the jail and shoot Matt Stone.'

'Jace, you can do any damn thing you want in that town from now on.' Braddock watched Caldwell's look of satisfaction. It was the perfect time to set his plan into motion. 'When you bring the money back, I'm going to Denver on business. I've made a few investments for you boys and I'm going to see that everybody gets a big bonus. It's time to start enjoying our profits.'

'There's been some grumbling about that,' Caldwell replied. 'The men also want some women up here.'

'Good idea, Jace. You tell them that when I get back from Denver they can have women here permanent.'

Matt and Spider did not take the usual route to Rattlesnake Canyon. The mountain trails were watched by the outlaws, and few riders ventured on them. They cut across country and wove their way through the foothills. They reached the mountains and found travel nearly impossible in the darkness. There was no trail to follow and their knowledge of the area was poor. But their biggest problem was the rough terrain. When they had gotten far enough away from town to feel safe they camped for what little remained of the night. They decided to sleep for about three hours, and then resume their journey. They did not light a fire.

The sun had been up for nearly an hour when the two men woke. The weather had been gradually warming the past few days, and they could tell it would be very hot today. They had a cold meal and continued their climb. They had chosen the south-western slope hoping to avoid detection by the outlaws. It would require additional travel, but this route reduced their chance of encountering gunmen. They spent the morning climbing through heavy growths of pine and other species. Many of the smaller trees grew at odd angles and clung awkwardly to the side of the mountain.

In the early afternoon they came to one of the many locations that required them to dismount and lead their horses up steep slopes. Even at the higher elevation, the midday sun beat down on them with intense heat. They finished a difficult climb and finally came on to a terrace that offered easier travel. Both men and horses were tiring from their efforts. Matt dismounted. 'Let's find some water and give the animals a breather.'

'The horses ain't the only thing that needs a rest,' Spider replied. 'This is one helluva tough mountain.'

Matt removed his hat and wiped the inside band with his bandana. Sweat rolled off his forehead and into his eyes, causing a slight sting. He replaced his hat. 'We haven't seen a soul up here and it's pretty easy to understand why. But at least it's safe.'

'So far,' Spider answered, wiping his brow. 'Let's find that water.'

They rode a short distance and found a small spring at

the far end of the terrace. A flow of clean water came out of a crack in a rock wall and formed a shallow pool at the base. The water then poured over the edge as a small creek and began its long journey to the valley below. After tending the horses, Spider walked toward Matt. 'Katie gave me your message in town but she didn't tell me how you escaped. What happened?'

Matt explained how Katie smuggled the gun into the jail.

Spider listened intently and when Matt finished, he shook his head. 'Well, I'll be darned! That Katie's sure something special.'

'She's that all right.' A smile came to Matt's face as he thought of the young girl, then he added, 'I wish I could have seen my face when that Colt fell on the floor. I couldn't believe my eyes.' The two men laughed as they began preparing their meal. They ate and decided to rest for half an hour. Matt grew quiet.

Spider watched his friend. 'All right. What are you thinking?'

'Rattlesnake Canyon. Everything points to the hideout being somewhere around there, but I can't figure it out. I've talked to several people about that place, and they all told me it's just swarming with rattlers. There's no possible way they could get horses in and out of there during the summer.'

'Maybe the hideout is just close to there.'

'I thought of that too, but we searched the area when we were tracking Jarrod's killers. There's nothing there.' Matt pondered the mystery. 'We're not too far from the canyon. Let's get moving so we can look it over before dark.'

It was late in the afternoon when the two riders neared Rattlesnake Canyon. They instinctively grew more cautious. When they were within walking distance to the mouth of the canyon they hid their horses and set out on foot. If they did run into snakes, they knew the horses would become excited and make excessive noise.

Both men carried rifles and they stayed along the edge of the steep mountain wall. When they were within sight of the canyon entrance they stopped to examine the surroundings. There was still no sign of anyone in the vicinity. Satisfied, Matt motioned for Spider to crouch and follow just behind. They had gone only a few feet when the eerie sound of a rattler's warning swept through the air. Matt carefully made his way around the snake's position and crept forward. They had gone only a few more feet when they heard two more snakes. Matt turned. 'Damn, Spider, we're not even in the canyon yet. This place is spooky.'

'Aw, hell, Matt, it's just a few little snakes. Nothin' to worry about.' Spider then took the lead as if to show Matt he could easily guide them through. He entered the canyon and had gone about ten feet when a six-foot diamondback struck at him from his left side. Spider jumped back just in time. 'I thought those things always shook their rattlers for a warning.'

It was becoming a serious situation, but Matt still let out a small laugh. Spider's attempt at taking charge did not last long. 'I like the way you handled that,' Matt said with a chuckle. He stopped for a few seconds. 'Listen to all those rattles. This place is crawling with snakes.'

Spider shook his head. 'I don't see any way those outlaws could be up in this canyon. It doesn't make sense.'

'I thought about it when we stopped at that spring,' Matt answered. 'I know Kimball was trying to tell the sheriff something when he mentioned this canyon. A dying man just wouldn't say something like that for no reason.'

'I know what you're saying, but I still don't see a bunch of outlaws going through here.'

Matt listened to the rattles and thought for a moment, then he motioned to Spider. 'Let's back outta here and figure this out.' The two men retraced their steps and went back into the trees.

They talked for a few minutes, then Matt suddenly grabbed his rifle and started off at a brisk pace. 'Come on. I've got an idea.' Matt stopped when he reached the horses. 'You usually carry some paper and a pencil in your saddlebags. You got any?'

'I think so. I'll check.' After a brief search, Spider produced a stubby pencil and a scrap of paper. 'What do you need these for?'

'I want you to go back to the ranch and gather the things on this list. Bring them back here, pronto.' Matt hurriedly scribbled several items on the paper and handed it to Spider.

Spider studied the list and his face took on a look of amazement. 'What in thunder do you need these for?'

'I'll explain when you get back. Just put those things on a pack horse and get them up here fast.' Matt glanced around. 'I'll hole up in those big rocks against that slope.'

After Spider left, Matt rode through the nearby area to make sure there was no one in the vicinity. He then went into the rocks and set up camp. He found a small patch of grass for his horse. Then he sat with his back against a large bolder and ate a cold meal. Except for the occasional sound of an animal, the night was hot and still.

Spider McCaw made good time during his ride down the mountain. It was early morning when he reached the ranch. He was surprised to find no activity around the barn and corrals, and became concerned when he realized that no one was performing routine chores. When he pulled to a stop, Major Colby came out of the house and stood on the porch. A Winchester leaned against the wall behind him.

Spider called out as he dismounted. 'What's wrong?'

'Nothing yet,' Colby said. 'Where's Matt?'

'He's safe. He's waiting for me at Rattlesnake Canyon.'

'Good, I've been worried.' Colby motioned toward the house. 'You look like you could use a good meal. We can talk inside.'

They got comfortable and waited for the cook to bring food. 'How come it's so quiet around here?' Spider asked. 'Where is everybody?'

Colby's tone turned sombre. 'I'll explain all that, but first I've got some bad news. Fuzzy's dead.'

Spider grimaced. 'What? How?'

Colby told of the incident at the knoll. He paused for a moment, and then added. 'He gave up his life for Laura.'

Spider was deeply saddened. 'I'm sure sorry, Major. There wasn't anybody who didn't like Fuzzy.'

'Except for Jace Caldwell and his bunch.'

The muscles in Spider's face tightened. 'It was Jace?'

'Yes, he—'

Spider interrupted, his tone cold. 'I've had it with that sonofabitch. I'm gonna kill him, Major. I'm gonna kill him stone dead.'

'There's more. Caldwell's not the leader of that gang. It's Fats Braddock. Do you know him?'

'I've seen him and I didn't like what I saw.'

'Well, he doesn't look like much, but he's resourceful and smart.'

'Anything else?'

'We may have gotten a break. Laura heard them say they were going to hit the banks in Everett and Benbow so I sent word to the sheriff and offered help. That's why all my men are gone. They've set up a trap in town. If those outlaws try the bank, it'll be their last job. I'm just worried they might delay for a while. I can't take a chance and

131

keep the men in town too long.'

Spider rushed through his meal and got up to leave. 'Matt's convinced that hideout's somewhere around Rattlesnake Canyon. I was supposed to bring some men back with these supplies.' He reached into his pocket and handed the small list to Colby. 'I know your boys are gone, but can you help me with this?'

Colby stared at the list with a confused expression. 'What's he want these for?'

'I don't know, but he's in a big hurry for me to get back.'

Colby shook his head. 'All right, but I still don't understand.'

They left the dining room and found Laura and Katie waiting in the front room. Katie ran to Spider as soon as she saw him. 'Is Mr Stone all right?'

'Well, Katie, thanks to you he is.' Spider looked at Laura and saw that her concerned expression had turned to one of relief. After the supplies were placed on a pack horse, Spider was ready to leave. He said goodbye to Laura and Katie, then spoke to Colby. 'You've only got one other hand here. Will you be OK?'

'I've got at least two men coming in from the east range. We'll be all right.'

Spider mounted a fresh horse. 'So long, Major. We'll be back as soon as we can.' He waved to Laura and Katie and set a course for the mountains.

At mid-afternoon, Spider left the foothills and began to climb the rugged slopes. He had purposely chosen a western route in hopes of avoiding contact with the outlaws, but it would be a difficult climb. The recent heatwave continued and forced him to rest the horses more often than usual. In an hour it would be dark. Spider hoped to reach Matt shortly after midnight and knew his goal would not be possible if there had not been a full moon. But even with the moonlight, travel was tedious. After a vigorous climb, he stopped to eat and rest the horses. He had expected nightfall to bring relief from the heat, but it remained warm. After twenty minutes, he was again climbing the mountain. It was nearly one in the morning when he reached Matt's camp. He greeted his partner and cared for his horses. He finished his task, then removed his bedroll and placed it opposite Matt's. 'Seen anything?'

'All quiet.'

Spider gave Matt the news from Colby and of the outlaws' plans to rob the two banks. After a brief discussion, they decided to go ahead with their current plans and then return to the ranch as soon as possible. But the news had given Matt a sense of urgency. 'Spider, I know you're real tired, but I think we should go into the canyon tonight. If we do find their hideout the dark will give us cover. If not, we can come back out when it's light. That way we can get back to the ranch a little quicker.'

'I don't mind. How soon?'

'You need an hour or two of sleep. I'll wake you.'

Spider crawled into his bedroll and then rose up on his elbows. 'What about those snakes? Will it be easier at night?'

Matt chuckled. 'Not this time of the year and with this heat. They'll be out looking for mates so they'll be downright active.'

CHAPTER 18

Matt woke Spider at three o'clock. After eating, Matt checked their gear. 'Let's see. Extra rope, rawhide, stove pipes, and an old sheet. Did you cut these pipes like I asked?'

'Yep, just like you said. Now, what are we going to do with them?'

'Hell, Spider, that's easy. We're going to put them over our legs.'

'What?' Spider sounded completely bewildered. 'You can't mean it?'

'We're going to walk right through those snakes.'

'Gawd, Matt, it won't work.'

'There's only one way to find out. Grab your things and let's get at it.' They packed their horses and led them as close to the canyon as possible. Spider mumbled to himself about snakes and stove pipes the entire way. When they stopped, Matt gave instructions to a very confused Spider McCaw. 'Take off your boots and wrap a long cloth strip around your knee and tie it down, but not too thick.' Matt finished with his wrap and picked up a length of pipe. 'Now put your foot through the pipe and pull it up over your knee. Use the short pipe first. Put the rawhide through the holes on top and tie them to your belt.'

Spider shook his head in disbelief. 'We've been

through an awful lot over the years but this beats everything.' He mumbled something inaudible and then continued his protest in a low voice. 'I swear, if a bunch of cowboys ever saw us wearing these contraptions. . . . Well, we'd just never hear the end of it.'

Matt took the longer section of pipe and pulled it up over the lower part of his leg. 'Believe me, this is going work.' He tried to put his boots back on, but failed. 'I was afraid of that but we can help each other with the boots.' After a short struggle, they were ready.

Spider tested his movement with the apparatus strapped to his legs. 'Matt, I don't mind the snakes so much, but what if we come up on eight or ten gunmen and have to make a run for it?'

Matt didn't answer for a moment. 'Sorry, I guess I didn't consider that.'

'Thanks, Matt. I can just see it now. Spider McCaw found dead with stove pipes strapped to his legs. Gawd all mighty!' He shook his head. 'One more question. What happens if I fall?'

'Don't.'

Spider cursed under his breath.

Matt stuck a piece of rawhide between his teeth, grabbed his rifle, and led off toward the mouth of Rattlesnake Canyon. Spider was slow to begin but he soon trudged along behind. The night was hot and still. The moon provided adequate light, and Matt found travel surprisingly easy because the stove pipes had been cut to just the right length. They were cumbersome, to be sure, but he was satisfied with his mobility while walking in a straight line. Moving sideways was a different matter.

Even before they entered the canyon, several snakes rattled warnings. Matt heard one to his right and instinctively tried to jump to the other side. The snake struck and missed, but if it hadn't been for a large shrub, Matt would have fallen. He steadied himself and waited for Spider. 'If you try to dodge you'll probably fall. I know it's instinct to jump from a striking snake, but we just can't do it. You've got to believe in the pipes.'

'Dammit, Matt, now I see why you wouldn't tell why you needed this stuff. You knew I'd never bring them back.' Just as Spider finished, a large diamondback struck from his right.

Thwack!

The snake's fangs hit the metal pipe and bounced off.

A split second later, another struck at Matt.

Thwack!

Matt found it nearly impossible to avoid an instinctive jump when the snakes lashed out and had to force himself to hold still. He had to trust the pipes. They moved a little farther when a seven-foot diamondback suddenly struck at Matt's right leg.

Thunk!

The huge snake's fangs went part way through the pipe and became stuck.

'Dang, Spider, look at this.' The huge reptile had struck just below the knee, and its fangs were embedded in the metal leggings. It swung wildly back and forth as Matt tried to shake it loose, but he couldn't dislodge the snake. He finally swung his rifle barrel down and attempted to pry the snake off the pipe.

They were in a dangerous spot, but Spider burst into laughter when he saw Matt trying to pry the huge snake from his leg with a Winchester. 'Lord, oh mighty . . . ain't that a sight!'

Matt was annoyed at first, but then he also started to laugh. After a few more attempts he managed to knock the snake loose. Both men found it hard to suppress their laughter. Matt whispered to Spider. 'We could be killed any minute and here we are laughing.'

Their mood quickly turned serious. There was work to be done and their lives were at stake. Matt took the lead and followed the canyon for several hundred yards. They could see only steep, jagged walls on either side. They stopped often in an effort to locate any possible exit from the canyon, but found none. Every few feet, the now familiar sound would ring out.

Thwack! Thwack!

There were so many strikes it would have been difficult to count them all, but with their hands held high, Matt and Spider had so far managed to avoid a skin-puncturing wound. They had entered the floor of the canyon against the nearest wall and were now gradually moving toward the centre. As they crossed the flatter middle portion, the two men encountered a considerable number of bones. It appeared that both men and animals had made the same ill-fated mistake. Many had gone into Rattlesnake Canyon never to be seen again.

Matt continued to search for a crevice or other passageway but found nothing. After they had gone halfway, Spider pointed toward a dark area to their left. Matt turned and saw a small crack in the rock wall. They changed course to investigate. The constant sound of rattlers seemed to ebb and flow each time they changed directions, but the sounds never stopped completely. But now, for the first time, there had been no strikes for several minutes and Matt began to relax. In an effort to avoid warning rattles to his left, he went around a large shrub and nearly stepped on a diamondback. The snake's strike caused him to jump to his right. He forgot his own advice and his reflexes instinctively took over. Matt felt himself falling but cumbersome pipes made it impossible to regain his balance.

He landed on a pile of dried bones that crumbled under his weight. He raised his head and found himself staring at the skeleton of a man, the skull just inches away. He glanced to his left and saw a huge rattler four feet away, coiled in the strike position – its tail vibrated as it gave the warning sound. Matt frantically tried to get up, but was unable because of the cumbersome pipes.

Spider stepped toward the snake and swung his rifle. The blow sent the snake back several feet. With the rattler safely despatched, he helped his friend get up.

Matt wiped his forehead. 'Whew, that was close.' He turned to Spider and put a hand on his shoulder. 'Thanks, pardner.' They were only a few feet from the crack now and safely made it to the wall. Matt peered at the gap. 'I don't think there's anything in here but we've got to check it.'

'It looks too hard for both of us to climb with these pipes on,' Spider said. 'I'm shorter and it will be easier for me.' He moved to the wall and put one leg up. 'Give me a hand and I'll see if I can get to that ledge.'

'All right. But don't take any chances.'

Spider chuckled and looked back at Matt. 'Look who's talking.'

Matt shook his head. 'Yeah, I know. Let me give you a hand.'

Spider made his way into the gap and disappeared.

Matt leaned against the wall and waited. Without further movement from the intruders, the turmoil in the canyon had died down and the snakes were quiet. Matt inspected his surroundings and noticed a large number of mice scurrying about the rocky wall. He had seen a few earlier, but thought little about the small creatures until now. Then it became clear. There must be a large population of mice and rats in the rocks. When they ventured into the canyon, they became food for the rattlers. Spider was gone for ten minutes. He reappeared and Matt helped him down. 'Find anything?'

'It's a dead-end. But the place is swarming with mice. They're everywhere.'

'Yeah, I saw a lot of them in the rocks. I think that's why there are so many snakes.' They made their way back toward the middle of the canyon and continued to search. The two men had travelled nearly the full length of the box canyon, but found no passage through the steep walls. With the closed end of the gorge now directly in front of them, Matt felt disappointed. Then he saw a dark area in the south-east corner, which he thought could be a large gap in the wall. He touched Spider's arm and motioned for him to follow. They climbed a gentle slope and Matt began to think they would no longer be in jeopardy from the snakes. There had been no attacks since they began to climb. They crossed rock-covered ground next to a small crest of dirt near the wall. A tremendous chorus of rattles rang out in front of them. The sound momentarily startled Spider and he lost his balance as small rocks slid under his boots. He started to fall into the small depression, but Matt grabbed him and shoved him back against the dirt ridge.

'Thanks. . . . That was close.'

They went around the small furrow and made their way to the wall. As they went by, two of the snakes slithered away, but two large ones remained, their rattles vibrating continuously as their bodies held the strike position. The crack in the wall was just above them, but Matt knew they could not reach it with the pipes strapped to their legs. He spoke quietly. 'Help me take off these boots. We're going to climb into this gap and have a look.'

With some effort they removed the pipes and started to climb the wall. Matt had gone only a few feet when he suddenly stopped. 'Let's hide these pipes. We'll need them to get out of here, and I'd hate for them to get into the wrong hands.' Matt found a small crevice in the wall to his right. He inspected the location, then told Spider to hand him the pipes and trappings, which he placed out of sight. He then slid an extra rope over one arm and around his body. They began to climb the wall. Matt reached a small ledge twelve feet above the ground while Spider was climbing a few feet to his right. Matt waited for his partner to catch up.

Spider reached for an adjacent, but lower ledge and began to pull himself up. Just as his head came even with the ledge something crawled on to his hand. He rose up slightly and came face to face with a giant tarantula. Spider yelled and jerked his hand from the ledge. The sudden movement caused him to fall backwards from the wall and he crashed into the ditch below, landing near two large rattlesnakes.

The impact sent the snakes into a coiled position.

Matt yelled to Spider. 'Don't move.' He picked up a large rock with both hands and manoeuvred to a position directly above the first snake. The moon provided enough light, but it was still risky. The snake was so close to Spider that he could easily miss and hit his partner. Matt wanted to take better aim but he knew there was no time. He dropped the heavy rock and watched anxiously as it fell.

Spider remained motionless as the rock plummeted down and landed on top of the snake. The crash and resultant vibration caused the other snake to strike. Spider lunged sideways just in time. The snake again coiled into the strike position.

Moving rapidly, Matt tied his rifle to the rope and began lowering it to Spider. They had earlier agreed not to use their weapons unless they were fired on but Matt had another idea. He called to Spider. 'Grab my rifle and club the sonofabitch.'

Spider reached ever so slowly for the rifle and took it by the barrel. He cautiously moved his arm back and held it there for a second, then called to Matt. 'OK, drop the rope.' The instant the rope landed, Spider swung the rifle and hit the snake just below the head. The impact propelled the reptile into the air causing it fall to the bottom of the slope. Spider lay back against the dirt and wiped his brow. Within seconds he had been inches away from his biggest nightmare – a huge tarantula; then he was nearly bitten by two large diamondbacks. He lay still for a time and stared at the moon.

Moments later, Matt helped his shaken friend up to the ledge. 'Are you all right?'

'I hurt my left wrist when I hit the ground but it'll be OK.' Spider shook his head. 'Jesus, did you see the size of that tarantula?'

Matt laughed. 'You just fell next to two of the biggest snakes I've ever seen and you're still worried about that spider.'

'I'd rather not go into it,' Spider said.

Matt nodded. 'Your rifle's right over there. Get it and we'll climb on up.'

Although the crack narrowed as they went higher, it also became less steep, and one man could easily make his way between the rocky walls. They continued on for several minutes until the gap suddenly ended. It was over an hour before sunup, but the moon provided sufficient light for them to see a basin below their position.

Matt pointed toward the buildings. 'Look what we've got down there.'

'By God, Matt, you were right. I'd bet a year's pay that's where the Mosquito Creek boys hang their hats.'

They surveyed the basin for several minutes, and then scanned the high walls on both sides of their location. Other than a dark area at the north end, there appeared to be no way in or out.

'I can see some horses down there,' Spider said, 'but it's

hard to tell how many.'

'I think there's only a few. I've got a feeling most of the gang must have gone to hit those banks. If there were twenty men down there we'd see a lot more horses.' Matt continued to study the area as he talked. 'But what I can't figure is how they get in and out of here. It must be through that dark hole.'

'Matt, if there's only a handful of men in here maybe we should take them.'

'That's why we're here. But first we've got to know how they get in. I think we can climb across and come in above that dark area.' Matt began to work his way along the wall. Movement was difficult at first, but it became easier when they reached a small terrace. Twenty minutes later, they stood directly above the dark hole. Matt had a better view of the corral from his new vantage point. 'I only see five horses. I think we should go over and wake those boys up.'

'How do we get down?'

'We'll use the rope and drop off right here. That way we can check out this hole first.' Matt secured his rope and then he looked toward the eastern sky. 'We'd better hurry. The sun will be up soon.'

CHAPTER 19

Matt lowered himself into the darkness. He descended over twenty feet until he stood on a rocky ledge on the edge of the fissure. He saw that it would be easy to climb down from this position. He tugged on the rope to signal Spider. After Spider reached the ledge, they climbed the short distance to the bottom and were surprised to find a horse tied at the edge of the wall. Their jump from the ledge startled the animal.

Matt calmed the horse. 'Whoa, boy . . . whoa.' They moved into the dark fissure.

'Why would they have a horse tied here?'

'Don't know,' Matt answered. 'But we're going to find out.'

At the spot where the moonlight was cut off by the overhang, the tunnel became pitch dark. They waited a moment to let their eyes adjust, but it did not help. Matt reached into his vest pocket and produced two matches. 'Let's go in a little farther and I'll strike a match. They moved down the slanted passage and came to the mine shaft. They reached the flat surface and Matt prepared to strike the matches. 'Here goes. Keep a look out.' He held the two matches together and struck them on his boot. They flared and lit up several feet around them. 'It's a mine shaft.'

Spider was puzzled. 'Where's the entrance?'

'I don't know. We've searched every inch of this mountain and we didn't find a shaft on this side.'

Spider peered into the darkness. 'This tunnel's got to come out somewhere.'

Matt squatted and looked at the floor. 'There have been an awful lot of horses through here.' The fire reached his fingers and he dropped the matches. 'I've only got a couple more matches. Did you bring any?'

'Yeah, I brought a bunch. I'll light one.' Spider lit a match and they moved a little farther.

'Up here,' Matt said. He found a torch, grabbed it, and held it out for Spider. It was made of cloth wrapped around a club. With the bright light given off by the flame they made their way to the other end of the tunnel.

They reached the large plank and the secret door. 'Will you look at this,' Spider said. 'Quite a set-up.'

'Yeah, they even put in new shoring. I still don't know how they hid the opening, but they obviously need this plank for something.' Matt pondered the wooden ramp for a moment. 'Damn, that's it. The tunnel entrance is too high; it's not where you'd expect to find it. Look at this. They lower the plank and the horses walk up the ramp and into the tunnel.'

'Now that we know how they get in here, let's go wake 'em up.' Spider, as always, seemed eager to get on with their mission.

They moved back through the shaft and Matt inspected the tunnel. When the torch was about to go out he whispered to Spider. 'There's another one up here.' Matt lit the new torch and looked around. 'I can see why they put up the new shoring. This old stuff is rotted.' He then examined the rocks the lumber supported. 'Look at those big cracks along the ceiling.'

Spider rubbed his chin. 'Are you thinking what I'm thinking?'

'Yeah, Spider, I think so. If we could pull down the shoring it looks like this whole section would collapse.'

'And they'd be trapped.'

'It looks like it. Unless they're smart enough to use stove pipes.'

'Not a chance,' Spider said. 'But how do we pull them down?'

'If we can get that horse in here without them hearing us we can use our rope and let the horse do the work. We'll be able to go out the hidden entrance by using that plank. If the ceiling doesn't collapse, we could use our rifles and hold them off from the trees. But if it does work, that whole gang will come back and they'll have nowhere to go.'

'I'll get the horse.' Spider started down the tunnel. He went through the fissure opening and stopped short at the sight of a light from one of the cabins. A voice sounded just in front of him.

'Charlie, is that you?'

Without answering, Spider walked toward the man with his rifle ready.

'Who's there?' the man asked.

As Spider approached the man the outlaw reached for his gun. The gunman's pistol had just cleared his holster when Spider's rifle butt connected with the outlaw's skull. The man fell backwards, but his finger had already squeezed the trigger. The gun roared skyward and the booming sound reverberated along the walls of the basin. Spider rushed to the horse, untied him, and then ran into the tunnel where he found Matt coming to help. 'I'll hold them off. Start on that shoring.'

Matt started to protest but Spider was already running back toward the basin.

Moving rapidly, Matt soon had the plank down and the horse in place. He tied the rope to a large shoring timber, then ran to the end of the tunnel and yelled at Spider. An exchange of gunshots sounded. 'Spider, let's move.'

Spider didn't answer for several seconds. He fired two shots at the gunmen, and then shouted at Matt. 'Go on. You'll have to pull four or five down before it goes. Do two or three, then I'll come.'

Matt knew Spider was right but he didn't like the idea of leaving his partner alone. He rushed back into the tunnel. His rope was already tied to the bottom of a new shoring timber at a critical point just inside the entrance. The timber gave way on the second attempt. There was some creaking and a few rocks fell, but that was all. Matt tied the rope to the new timber on the other side of the shaft. Again, the shoring came down, but only a few rocks fell. Gunshots continued as Matt secured the rope to one of the decayed supports. This wood gave way on the first try and an entire slab of rock crashed to the floor. He knew he couldn't attempt to pull more down without Spider. He ran through the thick dust and yelled. 'It's ready to go. Let's get out of here.'

Spider ran down the tunnel toward Matt's light. The two men crawled over the debris and got ready to pull another of the old supports down. Matt finished tying the rope and yelled at Spider. 'How many are up there?'

'There were at least five but two are down. The rest didn't seem too determined. I don't think they're too anxious to rush in here.'

'All right, let's try it.' Matt slapped the horse and sent him down the plank. A rumbling sound was quickly followed by a loud crashing noise from inside the old mining shaft. Seconds later, a cloud of dust billowed forth from the dark hole. The sun was just coming up as they stood outside and waited for several minutes as dust continued to spew from the tunnel.

'We'd better make sure,' Spider said.

'Let's be careful. Any movement might set it off again.' The torch had been put out and tossed aside, but a small amount of cloth was still attached to the wood. Matt lit the torch and they crept just inside the entrance. Much of the dust had settled, but it was still difficult to see.

Spider took the torch and inched his way into the shaft. He went about twenty feet and stopped. After a minute he came back outside. 'It's blocked. I don't know how thick it is, but it looks solid to me. I'd hate to be in their spot.'

'I'm not worried about them now,' Matt said, looking in the direction of Pine Valley. 'But there are still fifteen or twenty outlaws out there.'

'Yeah,' Spider replied. 'And I didn't see Caldwell in that hideout.'

Matt continued to look down the mountain. 'I don't like the idea of him being on the loose. I was going to let you rest some but I think we'd better head for the valley right away.'

'I'm all right,' Spider said.

They walked at a fast pace until they reached their hidden their horses. The sun had been up for two hours when they mounted and set out for the Box C.

The collapse of the mine shaft had driven the startled outlaws inside the basin into a state of terror. Each man had reacted in a different way but it quickly became every man for himself. They all knew there were still two exits out of the basin but they were both extremely hazardous. One exit was on the opposite side of the basin and involved a dangerous climb up the steep canyon wall, followed by a long walk down the mountain. The other passage required the men to cross the gap and walk through Rattlesnake Canyon. The perils of the two routes were quite different, but they were both potentially fatal.

Fats Braddock had always sought to be in control of

147

every situation, but as he rushed out of the blocked shaft his mind gave way to panic. The thought of being trapped inside the towering walls sent waves of horror through his mind. He hurried back toward his cabin and thought about the money he had been secreting in Denver. He had to get to his money – he had to. But how? Braddock entered his cabin and pulled up a board in the floor. He removed a small sack, grabbed a box of cartridges, and then went outside to get his men. They would help him, and he would pay them well. He would still be able to go to the East.

But when Braddock got outside there was no one in sight. He went to the bunkhouse and found it empty. Confused and angered he went outside. One outlaw sat against a rock, dying from a gunshot wound. He would be of no help and Braddock ignored him. Where were the others? They had to help him escape from the hideout that had suddenly become a prison. Braddock went behind his cabin and glanced around. Then he saw them. Two men were attempting to climb the southern wall. They were using ropes and were about a quarter of the way up. Braddock's size made it impossible for him to even consider this route. He became furious – his men had abandoned him.

He yelled at them but they either did not hear him or simply chose to ignore him. He shouted once more, but again there was no response. Without a second thought, Braddock raised his rifle and began firing on the men. When his first two shots fell short, he adjusted for distance and raised the barrel slightly. He fired two more times and one man appeared to be hit. The men scrambled along the wall and hid behind a rocky crag. With his targets now hidden, Braddock turned and looked about in desperation. He had to get to his money in Denver – it had all been planned so well. He thought for a moment, then blurted out loud. 'No damn snakes are going to keep me from my money.' With this proclamation, Fats Braddock headed straight for the gap that led to Rattlesnake Canyon.

After thirty minutes of difficult climbing he reached the crack and began to follow it out of the basin. Travel through the gap was relatively easy, even for such a large man. Once Braddock reached the other side and saw the canyon his feeling of panic eased. He thought he could easily manoeuvre through the area and he began to climb down the jagged wall. Without knowing it, he was within a few feet of the hidden stove pipes. He inched his way down using his hands and feet to hold on to the wall. He successfully made it to the same ledge where Matt had helped Spider from the snake-infested ditch.

Braddock's hands held on to the ledge as he sought footing below. He lodged one foot into a hole in the rock and began to work lower. It was then that he heard the eerie sound. Six large rattlesnakes were sunning themselves in the pit directly below. Their warning rattles sounded simultaneously. Braddock had been so intent on escaping that he had failed to inspect the ground below. With both hands still clinging desperately to sharp rocks, Braddock became horrified.

His hands were sweaty and he began to slip. He desperately sought to hang on, but gravity had become his enemy and his heavy weight was now a great burden.

Terror swept over Fats Braddock as his fingers began to slip from the ledge.

CHAPTER 20

Jace Caldwell had been waiting for this day. He felt the Mosquito Creek gang should have taken over Benbow long ago. Against twenty hardened gunmen, such a remote town would have little chance. He had reluctantly followed Braddock's orders, but he now had his chance. He would be given free run of the town. He had left the hideout the day before with eighteen men, and had camped overnight in the foothills about six miles from town. After the men ate breakfast, Caldwell sent half of them to rob the bank in Everett. He would use the remaining men for his assault on Benbow. Including himself, he would have a raiding party of ten hardened gunmen. While six men robbed the bank, Caldwell would take the other three with him to the jail. If the sheriff was there, Caldwell intended to shoot him on the spot. But his primary mission was to kill Matt Stone.

Caldwell instructed his men to split into two groups. The larger band would enter town from the south and go directly to the bank. Caldwell and three others would come in from the north and stop at the sheriff's office. The outlaws rode together until they were two miles from Benbow, then they separated as planned. It was noon when Caldwell stopped at the edge of town. He observed the street for several minutes, then signalled his men forward. The four men spread apart and sent their horses in at a walk. Caldwell continued to watch the street but everything appeared normal. He reached the jail, glanced toward the bank and saw his men getting into position. They had orders to hit the bank when he entered the sheriff's office. Caldwell scanned the area, then gave the signal. Two men followed him into the office while the third stood guard outside.

He found a deputy behind the sheriff's desk, but there was no one else in the room. Caldwell spoke in a matter of fact tone. 'Where's the sheriff?'

'He ain't here, Jace.'

'I can see that. Where is he?'

'He went down the street. I reckon he was going to eat.'

Without another word, Caldwell drew his pistol and shot the lawman in the chest. Except for a look of disbelief on the wounded man's face, he did not move. Caldwell then shot him through the forehead. The deputy fell backwards – a dead man before he hit the floor. Caldwell hurried across the room and opened the door to the jail. He had waited years for his chance to kill Matt Stone, and he meant to enjoy the opportunity. He took two steps into the jail and saw no one. He ran to the next cell and yelled, 'Where the hell is he?'

A barrage of gunfire sounded from the street. Caldwell spun around and ran into the office. The shooting from outside became continuous. As Caldwell ran toward the door he realized the gunfire was much heavier than it should be. He pushed one of his men aside and shouted, 'What's going on out there?'

The man who was standing guard outside ran through the office door at the same instant and nearly bumped into Caldwell. 'Jace—'

Anger boiled inside the big gunman. 'What's all the shootin'?'

'The whole street exploded down there. There are men firing from everywhere.'

Caldwell looked down the street and saw two of his men on the ground. Two more appeared to be trapped in the bank under heavy fire. One of his men was hunched over his saddle and riding hard toward the sheriff's office. Caldwell ran to the edge of the boardwalk and shouted at the man. 'What happened?'

The rider was too far away to hear.

Caldwell waited a few seconds and repeated his call.

The man pulled his horse to a violent stop. 'It's a trap. They were waitin' for us. Let's get outta here.'

Furious, Caldwell headed for his horse. 'How'd they know?'

'I don't know, Boss, but there's a whole lot of Box C men down there.'

Caldwell swung into his saddle, overcome with rage. 'Colby, it's got to be Colby.' Several shots suddenly came in their direction. A bullet dug into the post not far from his head. Caldwell spun his horse around and looked toward the bank. 'If all of his men are in town there can't be many at the ranch.'

'What're we gonna do?'

The big gunman turned his horse away from the bank. 'I'll tell you what we're gonna do. We're going to Colby's place.'

'The Box C?'

'Yeah, I'm gonna kill Colby and burn his place to the ground. You boys can have his women.' Several more shots whined up the street past the five outlaws. 'Let's get the hell out of here.' They rode out of town and turned east toward the Box C Ranch.

CHAPTER 21

It was late afternoon when Matt Stone and Spider McCaw left the main trail to Benbow. Their new route would allow them to exit the mountains closer to the Box C Ranch. An hour later, they rode through the last stand of trees and approached a point that offered a panoramic view of Pine Valley. The narrow path required them to ride in single file until they came out on to a small terrace. After thirty yards they could see most of the valley.

Spider rode across the terrace, then suddenly stopped. He sounded a loud groan.

Matt yelled to him, 'What's wrong?'

'Aw, hell, Matt. Look.'

Matt turned and saw it. The Box C Ranch was visible from the edge of the terrace and it was on fire. He could tell it had not been aflame too long. Heavy smoke was just beginning to billow skyward. Matt's heart sunk. A picture of Jarrod Kern's dead body flashed through his mind. Not again, he thought . . . not again.

The two men spurred their horses and raced toward the valley floor. Matt's mind pictured each member of the Colby family as he charged down the trail. He thought of the major, of Katie, and of Laura. The possibility of them lying dead beneath tattered blankets sickened him. The vision caused him to whip his horse incessantly as he dashed ahead of Spider.

As he began to draw away, Spider yelled at him. 'Ease up, Matt. The horse can't take it.'

It was still a long way to the ranch, and Matt's fear for the Colbys had overtaken his senses. He realized what he was doing and slowed the animal's speed to a sustainable pace. A mile from the ranch, he pulled his rifle from the boot and looked toward the flaming house. The memory of the burning Kern ranch and Jarrod's body again swept through his mind. His heart pounded as he rode. Even with the wind rushing by, he broke into a cold sweat.

Matt glanced back and saw Spider veering off to his right, about twenty yards behind. His partner obviously did not want to charge into the ranch yard too close together. That would make them easy targets. At six hundred yards from the house, Matt's horse was tiring badly. But it was not far now. The horse laboured as he rode up and stopped behind the barn. He then moved cautiously along the wall and entered the yard.

There was no one in sight. Matt feared the Colbys were caught in the inferno. He started to approach the house, but his horse shied from the heat and flames. The house was now fully engulfed. If the Colbys were inside he knew it was too late unless they had found somewhere else to hide.

'The barn!'

He started toward the building when he heard someone yell. He looked through the yard and saw Spider about a hundred yards away, bent over a body on the ground. Matt spurred his horse. As he rode toward Spider, he saw another body fifty yards farther out. The man appeared to be dead. Matt pulled to a stop and saw that the man on the ground was Gus Knox. A Winchester lay a few feet away.

Spider looked up. 'He's been shot twice, but it doesn't

look too bad. One in the arm, one in the leg.'

Matt spoke to the injured man as he dismounted. 'Where are the Colbys?'

Knox rose to his elbows and pointed to the east. 'They rode off that way. Jace Caldwell's after them. I held them off long enough for Colby to get his girls and leave, but they didn't have much of a head-start.'

Matt put his foot in the stirrup and started to mount his horse.

Spider looked up and yelled. 'Matt, wait. Our horses are done in.' He turned back to Knox. 'How many of them?'

'Five, but I got one. He's lying over there. You two go on. I'm all right.'

Matt swung into the saddle. 'Come on.'

Spider spoke briefly to Knox, then followed Matt toward the barn.

Matt ran into the building, intent on getting any fresh horse. It was then he remembered Mesquite, a horse Colby had bred for speed. Matt led the big black out and began to saddle the animal. Spider followed suit with the other horse. Minutes later, they burst out of the barn astride the two of the fastest horses in the territory. Matt considered the right pace for the horses as he set a course in the direction Knox had indicated. Normally, he would not have gone out too fast for fear of fatiguing the animals before catching the killers. But Mesquite and the other horse had great endurance, and the Colbys were in severe danger. Matt put Mesquite to a gallop across the flats.

The wind stung his face as he rode. Different images flashed through his mind. But most of all, there was fear. He already knew what Caldwell was capable of doing to a man, but he shuddered over what the thug might do to Katie and Laura. The visions propelled him onward in a near desperate state. Mesquite was game and responded to Matt's urging. Matt raced across the flats, searching ahead, but he saw no one.

Because of the large number of tracks near the ranch, it was difficult to pick out fresh marks. Instead of trying to find the tracks, he remained intent on going in the direction Knox had pointed. As they got farther away it would be easier to pick up fresh markings.

Minutes went by and Matt continued to scan ahead, but still he saw nothing. He became concerned about the horse's pace and slowed the animal slightly. There was a sudden rumbling of gunfire in the distance. He concentrated on listening. Again he heard the noise. A distant boom sounded – then another. Matt slowed to pinpoint the location. The shots were coming from his right, toward the foothills. He turned Mesquite and looked for his partner. Spider was not far behind and closing. Matt pointed toward the hills and spurred his horse. Spider had angled his horse to the right when he saw Matt's signal and the two soon rode abreast.

Matt searched ahead and shouted, 'I heard shots but I can't see anything.'

Spider pointed. 'Over there.'

Matt's eyes swept to his right and fell on several horses bunched together, but he could not see anyone. They were still too far away. He called to Spider. 'We'd better spread some . . . but not too far.' They grew closer to the horses and could now hear a barrage of gunshots. When they were within range, Matt signalled for Spider to pull up. Matt stopped next to a large rock, dismounted, and grabbed his rifle. 'That's Caldwell's bunch. They must have Colby pinned down.'

'I can't hit 'em from here,' Spider shouted.

'Your carbine won't but my rifle will,' Matt placed his .45–75 Winchester on the rock. 'I told you a seventy-five load would come in handy.' Matt took careful aim and fired at the distant target. He watched the effect, adjusted his aim, and then continued to shoot at regular intervals. He paused just long enough to concentrate on his target. After his third shot, the outlaws returned his fire. But their carbines were inaccurate at this distance. Matt continued to squeeze off shots until his gun was empty, then he began reloading.

Spider had been squinting at the target. 'It's hard to tell, but I think you hit one or two. Either that or you shook them up real good. They're damn sure moving about.'

Matt finished loading and went to his horse. 'Let's go.'

'Are you just gonna charge right in?'

Matt tugged on his hat. 'Hell, yes.'

'All right, but let's spread out.'

'I think we've got them in a cross-fire,' Matt said. 'Colby must be shooting at them from the other side. I'm going straight in. You veer off to the right.' Matt pulled an extra pistol from his saddlebags and shoved it under his belt. He then reached into his pocket and pulled out a short strip of rawhide, which he stuck between his teeth. He spurred Mesquite and chewed on the strip of hide. Matt set a course directly toward the outlaws. After fifty yards, he saw one of the four horses run off without a rider. Then two men suddenly jumped on to their horses and raced off in opposite directions. He was now close enough to see that one of them was much larger than the other. It had to Jace Caldwell.

But there were four men. After a few more yards he saw one man sprawled on the ground. Another rose to his knees and began firing. Matt pulled the gun from his belt and continued to bear down on the outlaw. The whine of a bullet zipped past Matt's ear. He raised his revolver and fired. A miss – he fired again. His second shot caught the man in the head and hurled him on to his back. Matt looked across the flats, but still could not see the Colbys.

Where were they? Fear for their safety again swept over Matt. He looked toward Spider and signalled for him to stop and search the area. As soon as he knew Spider understood, Matt sent Mesquite racing after Caldwell. The black had been running hard for some time, but Mesquite had exceptional stamina. Matt also knew Caldwell's horse could not have rested long after chasing the Colbys, but Matt still wondered if Mesquite could hold up. He bent low behind the neck of the black horse and chased after the gunman.

Gradually, the distance began to shorten. Mesquite showed tremendous courage. Again, the distance narrowed. Matt could now see Caldwell glancing back every so often. He seemed to know he would be caught. Mesquite continued to gain on the outlaw. At five hundred yards, Caldwell suddenly stopped and turned his horse around.

Matt stared at the big gunman. What was he up to?

Jace Caldwell then sent his horse into a gallop – straight at Matt.

In that instant, Matt knew one of them had only minutes to live.

The two men charged toward each other. Matt pulled the pistol from his holster and replaced it with the weapon he had been using. He wanted a fully loaded gun.

At two hundred and fifty yards, neither man had discharged his weapon. The distance narrowed.

At one hundred and fifty yards, Caldwell fired once. The bullet went wide.

Matt held his fire.

Caldwell fired again. The bullet whined past Matt's head.

Still he waited.

The two horses were now closing in on one hundred yards. Matt raised his gun and fired his first shot. The moment he discharged his weapon, a bullet caught the top of his hat and sent it spinning through the air. They grew closer and Matt could now see the killer's face. Each man continued firing, but neither hit his target.

Matt had two shots left.

Caldwell threw his pistol aside and pulled another. He was firing rapidly now.

A bullet whistled above Matt's head as he squeezed the trigger, but Caldwell had leaned to one side and the bullet missed. The two men were nearly on top of each other now, and Matt saw Caldwell take aim. Smoke erupted from the outlaw's pistol as he charged forward.

Matt had one shot left. He had been leaning over until now, but he suddenly rose straight up in his saddle and fired his last shot. The bullet ripped through Caldwell's chest and the big man fell heavily to the ground. Matt pulled to a stop and reached for his rifle.

He glanced toward the outlaw. Jace Caldwell lay motionless twenty yards away.

Matt dismounted and slowly walked toward the gunman. His instinct told him the man was dead, but he would not drop his guard until he knew for sure. He approached cautiously and rolled the man over with the gun barrel. Jace Caldwell was dead.

Matt immediately became concerned for the others and looked toward where he had left Spider. He saw a single rider coming straight at him from his left.

At first he couldn't see who it was. Then he knew – it was Laura Colby. Matt moved away from the dead body and waited. Laura pulled to a stop and dismounted. Tears flowed down her cheeks as she ran to Matt. Their embrace was charged with emotion.

When they finally released, Matt looked across the valley. 'Katie? Your father?'

'They're all right. We hid in a gully and fought back.

Dad told Katie to run as far up the gully as she could and hide.'

'Where?'

Laura pointed behind Matt. 'Over there.'

Though the outlaws were no longer a concern, Matt was still worried about Katie. They ran to the gully and looked down. It was empty. They went along the edge and searched the small ravine. They both saw her at the same time.

A nine-year-old girl with freckles on her nose suddenly climbed out of the gully about forty yards away. When Katie saw Matt and Laura she ran straight toward them. Matt and Laura crouched down next to each other. Katie ran between them and threw her arms around each of their necks.

Katie held on tight. She knew they were safe now – she had seen it in Matt's eyes. But she still clung to them as she looked across the valley. There were tears in her eyes and a smile on her face.

At that same moment, a large hawk soared high over Rattlesnake Canyon. Gliding smoothly, the bird's wings tipped slightly to one side, then to the other while its keen eyes searched for prey. The hawk seemed to float effortlessly through the warm air.

Far below lay the swollen body of a man, a dozen snake bites were spread over his body. The dead man was Fats Braddock.